# *NO REGRETS*

# NO REGRETS

## By
## Michele Murry

E-BookTime, LLC
Montgomery, Alabama

# NO REGRETS

Copyright © 2005 by Michele Murry

All rights reserved. No part of this book may be reproduced or transmitted in any form or by any means, electronic or mechanical, including photocopying, recording, or by any information storage and retrieval system, without permission in writing from the copyright owner.

This is a work of fiction. Names, characters, places and incidents either are the product of the author's imagination or are used fictitiously, and any resemblance to any actual persons, living or dead, events, or locales is entirely coincidental.

Library of Congress Control Number: 2005934659

ISBN: 1-59824-084-6

First Edition
Published October 2005
E-BookTime, LLC
6598 Pumpkin Road
Montgomery, AL 36108
www.e-booktime.com

# Dedication

To my sons, Jeremy and Justin, you'll never know how deep my love is for you. No matter what hard times come in life...no regrets. And to my friends, Dawn and Lorna, your encouragement and belief in me have enabled this book to come about.

# Introduction

Victoria Livingston was conscious for now, a state that was getting more rare with each new day. She watched Sarah as she checked the IV pump, listening to the soft, steady beat of the machines. Victoria was thankful for the medicine that kept the pain at bay, but it made her feel foggy. She knew her time was running very short and she didn't want to spend it in a hazy daze. Her life had only consisted of forty-nine short years. There was so much to think about. Had she lived her life in a way that she could be proud of? When she passed over and stood before God, she wondered if she would hear those words she had dreamed of all of her life...well done My good and faithful servant.

Her children had visited her yesterday. How she wished she could spend more time with them. Did they know how much she loved them? Did they understand how hard she had tried to be a good mother? She had always felt awkward as a mother, almost as if she were living a part she was not meant to play. It wasn't that she didn't love her children - she loved them more than she had ever loved anyone, including herself. She had wanted to tell them things about her life for many years, but what would they think of her then? Would they understand or think less of her? She didn't know where she

# Introduction

could possibly begin in explaining what had been her crazy, sometimes whimsical, sometimes scary life. Would they understand the very misunderstood disease that drove her most of her life? She just didn't think she could face one more day if they looked at her with disappointment in their eyes. The weight of guilt and shame weighed heavily on her chest now. Would they ever forgive her for the life she had led them through?

"Is there anything else I can do for you right now, Ms. Victoria?" Sarah's voice had a light southern lilt that always soothed her. She knew that Sarah was paid to take care of her, but there was a gentleness in her eyes that told Victoria that she wasn't just there for the money. She was called to take care of people, and she took her calling very serious. She truly was there to serve Victoria, which was why Victoria knew Sarah would help her. "Yes, Sarah, there is something else you can do for me." This was a long time coming. It was time to be completely open and honest with her children.

# Chapter 1

Abigail was the oldest of the three children. She was the responsible one, the one who usually took care of everything. She wished she could be the one who was taken care of now. It wasn't that she enjoyed being in charge, it just seemed that the responsibility was always handed to her by some invisible being that disappeared before she could realize what was happening. Had she had the chance, there were many times when she would've handed it back and ran as fast as she could. Sitting here on her mother's porch was one of those times.

She was barely thirty and had practically raised her two half siblings, Bailey and Patrick, and sometimes her own mother. Now she was being the responsible one that took care of her mother while she was dying at forty-nine years old. She loved her mother, truly she did. There were times when she felt so close to her and safe and loved, but then there were times when she barely recognized her mother. What happened to her during those times? Sometimes Abigail felt as if maybe she had done something to drive her mother deep within herself, into

## Michele Murry

her room for days at a time. Those times worried Abigail more than any other. Those were the times when she could not get her mother to eat. She couldn't get her to get up and get dressed or go to work. She would try to talk to her mother, but all she would talk about is everyone being better off if she were dead.

Abigail would take care of the house and the children and then lock herself into her room at night, praying for God to bring her mother back to her. "It's not fair!" she would cry out, "I'm only a young girl. How could You let this happen to me? What is happening to my mother? What will become of me?" She would exhaust herself crying out in her pain.

Her mother had always taken them to church. She knew her mother had a personal and deep relationship with God. So how could her mother do this to them? Why wasn't her faith strong enough to get her through? Abigail harbored ill feelings towards her mother sometimes. It made her feel guilty to do so, but why should she be the one to raise this family? She felt like she had given up so much over the years. She hadn't taken the scholarship to UCLA that had been her dream. Instead she chose to stay at home and attend the Junior College one town over. Bailey and Patrick were still in need of someone to watch over them and take care of them, and she wasn't sure her mother could handle that if she went away.

There was also Adam. How she had loved this man. They met at college and dated quite a bit for over a year. But once again her mother had taken to the bed, for over a month this time, and it became clear to Abigail that her mother needed her. Adam had told her that he could wait. He told her that he understood. How could he pos-

## No Regrets

sibly understand when she couldn't even understand it herself? There was something deeper bothering her about it, too. What if. Oh, the what if's ate at her heart sometimes. What if she were like her mother? How could she ask someone else to take care of her the way she had taken care of her mother? It wouldn't be fair. She vowed never to have children, afraid of what she might impose on them.

She had become an accountant after college, enjoying the stable, steady, humdrum existence of her job. She went to work, came home, fed her cat, and watched TV. Wasn't that what normal was? She enjoyed knowing what to expect when she got home, never having to wonder what scene she would find waiting for her.

The pangs of guilt started stabbing at her heart. Again, it wasn't that she didn't love her mother. It wasn't even that her mother hadn't taken good care of them. She knew her mother had done the very best she could.

She remembered back to the good times. Her mother would be feeling so good and full of energy after one of her bed episodes that it would be non-stop fun for a while. She couldn't be sure if it was out of guilt or from sheer relief of the episode being over. The house would always be filled with the sweet smells of all kinds of pastries and cookies and pies, and they would all stay up late playing games together and listening to mother read to them in her soft, drawn out southern accent. They would usually get new clothes during this time, new things for the house, sometimes even a new car! She was so thankful to have her mother back, that she really didn't care about all of that. She was just proud to have someone take care of her for a while.

## Michele Murry

Things would finally get back to normal for a period of time. Mother would be working hard at some new job she had taken when she would resurface from her room and once again life would be normal.

Sometimes Mother would start dating someone she would meet from work. Abigail seldom liked them. She thought most of them were rude to her mother and to them, as well. She would hear them fight every once in a while when they would come home and think that everyone was asleep. She had heard a couple of them hit her mother a time or two. It was so hard to stay put in bed. Her mother may not have been perfect, but she didn't deserve that.

Abigail tried several times to talk to her and tell her she deserved better, but she always had this sad, faraway look in her eye. After she left Patrick's dad, it was if she had given up all hope of ever having true love. She seemed so hungry for love, but settled for anything she could get. At least she wasn't making the mistake of marrying them all anymore.

Abigail's father was her mother's high school sweetheart. She had told her many stories about how they were best friends, but should've never been married. Her father, Dillon Westbury, left for the Army not long after they separated. She was only three at the time, so she couldn't remember him. He was headed over to Vietnam to help bring back MIA's when his plane crashed. They said it was some sort of freak accident. All she knew was that she no longer had a dad.

She had felt like Bailey's dad really loved her. He never treated her any differently than he did her younger sister and always tried to include her into his life. She didn't much care for the way he treated her mother, but at least he didn't hit her like some of the others did. Bailey still sees her dad fairly regularly, but after the divorce he never even asked about Abigail again.

Patrick was the youngest of the three. His dad, Blake Ashen, what can one say about him? He was fine at times, until you did one little thing that he deemed wrong. You had better watch out then. He would get violent with whomever was around. Victoria had told him she would take it, but wouldn't stand for it when it came to her children. Abigail really wished she wouldn't have taken it for herself, either. His dad left just a few weeks before Patrick was born.

Sarah quietly came out on the porch where Abigail had been sitting on the porch swing, swept away in her thoughts. Abigail reached up to take the glass of lemonade that Sarah held out to her and moved over so Sarah could join her on the swing.

"How is she today," Abigail said, still trying to pull herself out of the past and into the present.

"She's in pain, but I think her heart hurts more than her body," said Sarah.

"I don't understand."

"She's worried about you, you know. She's worried about how you feel about her. She's worried about how you will be when this is all over."

Abigail's eyes filled with tears, but her jaw stayed as taunt as ever. "She knows I love her."

"Yes, but do you love yourself?"

"What?" Abigail turned to Sarah, staring at her, trying to figure out what she meant by that. "I'm not the one who has lived my life in disrespect to myself and my children!" The words were out there before she could retract them.

Sarah didn't even flinch. She just reached out and gently took Abigail's hand. "It's okay," she whispered.

Abigail felt so guilty! How could she have even one bad thought about her mother when she was lying in there dying? That strong set face of determination started to melt. She could no longer hold back the tears. "I'm sorry. I'm so very sorry, mother. Oh, please know that I love you," the sobs were soft, barely audible.

"Abigail," Sarah spoke softly, "Your mother knows how hard it has been for you. I think someday you'll understand from her point of view, but right now she just wants you to lean on God. It's okay to feel the emotions. It's okay to tell God you don't understand. Just please do this one thing for your mother now, let go of the bitterness."

"How can I, Sarah? I know that God loves me, but I can't understand why my life has been the way it was and is now. I can't understand how God could take my father from me, and now my mother. I don't know, Sarah. It's going to be hard for me to trust God on this one. I need answers." Abigail got up and walked to the porch railing, staring out into the green grass that had been freshly mowed. The sun was so bright that she had to squint to even look out at the world beyond the cover of the porch.

Sarah stood and walked to where Abigail leaned against the porch railings. She gently put her hand on Abigail's back and said, "God will give you the answers you seek, but for now you have a mother in there that needs to see your face, needs to feel your touch."

"You're right," Abigail said as she wiped her face on the sleeve of her cardigan. She took a deep breath, whispered a quick prayer and went to see her mother.

## Chapter 2

Bailey was cruising down the Interstate with her music blaring and her long blonde hair whipping around in the car from the lowered windows. She was singing at the top of her lungs and serenading the other cars as she passed by them. She laughed as she remembered her sister, Abigail, once calling her the dramatic one. Oh well, it was better than being so stiff necked all the time like Abigail. If there was one thing Bailey's mother had taught her, it was to live life to the fullest and follow your dreams.

She tried to let the thought of her mother fly right on out with the chewing gum wrapper she had just flung out the window, but it was getting harder each day to not think about her. Bailey was only twenty-five, how could she be losing her mother to cancer? Her mother was so young and vibrant for forty-nine. Even still, as she sped down this Interstate that would lead her to her mother's house, trying very hard to hang on to the whimsical feelings of life her mother had passed on to her, she knew that it was true. Shortly her mother would be gone.

She would not be sad though. That word was not in her vocabulary. She refused to let it in now. Her father would sometimes playfully say she was as crazy as her mother. She refused, of course, to believe he meant anything bad by that, and would just smile and start bowing and blowing kisses as if he had just given her rave reviews for a leading part she had just played.

Her father was Troy Townsend, bank president of a major bank in the city. She loved her father, but he reminded her a lot of Abigail sometimes, so serious and never knowing how to let go and relax. You also had to be careful around him sometimes. If something had gone wrong down at the bank that day he was capable of biting off your head, chewing it up and spitting out your teeth. She didn't like being around him during those times, so she made sure she planned visits that were in public and in upbeat places, ensuring a pleasant visit.

Her mother never said a word about her father, but Bailey wondered sometimes if he had taken out his frustrations on her back then. Her father said he left because her mother was crazy. Abigail had said it was because he cheated on their mother repeatedly. Mother never said a word, just seemed to accept whatever came.

Bailey thought herself a lot like her mother. They both loved to have fun and throw caution to the wind. There were days when her mother couldn't join her in her adventures for the day, but Bailey understood that she was sick. Her mother would always come right back when she was feeling better again and off they would go to the farthest depths of their imagination and become exotic creatures and superstars.

Bailey figured the trait of adventure and excitement she had gotten from her mother was the catapult that

## No Regrets

launched her career as a dress designer. Bailey just finished college and was now working for one of the largest design firms in Texas. She was on her way. Nothing could stop her.

Of course, this set back of mother's cancer wasn't helping her get started the way she had hoped. She had missed a lot of work trying to go to the small remote town of Criar, where her mother now lived, to visit with her as much as possible. Bailey tried not to think of the end being near, but it was. Her mother had been so small and weak the last visit. But if there was one thing that her mother had taught her it was this, God is in control.

Bailey was putting all of her trust in that one statement. She hadn't had her mother for near as long as she would've liked to, but she knew that her mother was settled and ready to meet her Maker whenever He said it was time.

Bailey thought back a minute at seeing her mother in church. Her mother was a mix of regal beauty and whimsical dramatics. She really thought her mother went for the shock factor sometimes, which Bailey just loved about her. She could almost hear her mother's voice, singing in church, now. It was a rich, smoothing voice that could shake the rafters. Who would've ever thought that a woman of such small stature could have such a strong voice.

Bailey realized that the miles had flown by and she was already pulling into her mother's driveway. As she had turned in she saw Sarah, mother's nurse, standing on the porch, looking thoughtful.

"Hello, Sarah!" Bailey exclaimed in that dramatic way of hers.

"Hello to you, too, Bailey." Sarah grinned. Sarah

loved the air of hope and laughter that Bailey brought into a room with her presence. "How was your trip?"

"Oh, you know, sang to an old couple I passed, waved at a few truckers, made faces at a few kids."

"That's our Bailey," Sarah said with a laugh.

"How is she today?"

"Weak. Your sister is with her right now."

"Then I'll give them a few minutes before I go in."

"Come, sit with me then." Sarah said, sitting back down on the swing.

Bailey tossed her bags over by the door and sat down beside Sarah. Sarah watched her face as she began to push the swing back and forth with her feet. "How are you doing with all of this, Bailey?"

"To be honest, I'm not sure how I feel right now or even how I'm supposed to feel. Does that make sense?"

"With you it does," Sarah teased.

"I'm crushed at the thought of losing my mother, but there's this peace that I can't explain that God has given me. I don't want to lose her, but I don't want her to hurt anymore, either."

"That makes perfect sense. I'm going to ask you to do something for me and for your mother. I'm going to ask you to please be patient and understanding with your sister this weekend. She is struggling with a lot of things that she really needs to deal with. She needs your help."

"What can I do, besides not be as annoying as I like to be with her?"

"We both know that Abigail has given her heart to God, but I'm not sure that she always lets Him have the reins to her life. She has had to be so responsible in helping your mother during the times when she was sick and help with raising you and your brother, I'm not sure that she knows how to give these hurts to God. Can you please be there for her?"

"Of course. I know I play around a lot and pretty much everything is made into a joke, that's how I handle my pain, but I want this to be a time of remembering the good times that we had with our mother. I want us to peacefully hand her over to God, knowing that He will take care of her. I especially want Abigail to let go of the past. If she could just learn to give things to God, truly give them to Him, then maybe she wouldn't always have that 'my pantyhose are two sizes too small' look on her face."

Sarah just shook her head.

"Have you heard from Patrick, yet?" asked Bailey.

"Yes. He called about two hours ago. He should be here shortly."

Just then Abigail emerged from the house. She had such a defeated look, a burdened look, that all Bailey could do was stand and hug her sister. She made no jokes, or crass remarks, just held her. She thought she might have even felt a couple of silent sobs as she held her sister, but soon Abigail released Bailey and that tight, in control look was back on her face.

Abigail walked off the porch and Bailey started to follow after her, but Sarah put her hand on her arm and gave her a look that said, 'Let her go.'

"I think I'll go see mother now. Please let me know when Patrick gets here." Bailey said as she opened the squeaky screen door.

"I will. Let me know if there's anything your mother needs."

Sarah sat back down on the swing and began to

## Michele Murry

move it with her toe. She closed her eyes and let the breeze blow through her hair as she cried out to her best friend. "God, please help this family. They are all so different, but their need is the same, You. I have no doubt that you sent me to Ms. Victoria for a reason. May Your will be done in this house, in this family."

Her thoughts were interrupted by the roaring sound of Patrick's truck. "Why guys think the louder, the better, I'll never know."

# Chapter 3

Bailey may have been dramatic, but Patrick could outdo her drama with his wildness any day of the week. He was twenty-three, handsome, and a rebel.

Patrick was the only one of the three children who didn't believe in God. They had all talked to him many times, but he said he couldn't believe in a God that would let his dad just disappear.

They had tried to explain to Patrick that each person has to make their own decisions in this life, and for whatever reasons his dad had for leaving, it wasn't God's choice, it was his father's. For whatever reason or whomever's choice, Patrick didn't like it, nor accept it. His mother had tried to tell him that his father loved him very much. She said that, however misguided, his father left because he thought it was the best decision for Patrick. What she hadn't told him was that his father was a drug addict who had tried to get off of the drugs several times, but failed. It didn't matter to Patrick what excuse anyone gave him. The fact was, he didn't have a father that cared enough to stick around. He hadn't even used his father's name, didn't want to. He used his mother's maiden name which she had taken back. Patrick knew his mother and sisters believed in God and spent their time in Bible studies and such, but he would rather spend his time at the club with his buddies. They were always there for him like clockwork. Buy them a drink and they would be your buddy forever, or at least the next day. That was okay, too, because it meant that he didn't have to stick around for them either.

Patrick strutted up the front steps like a peacock trying to show off its pretty tail feathers to Sarah. She was older, but not that much. He could handle having an older woman around, he thought smugly.

Sarah watched him strut, but didn't let out the laugh that was building up inside of her. Abigail came walking around the side of the house just then. Sarah was thankful she wouldn't have to spend that time with Patrick alone. She was forever having to try to tell him, politely, why it would be a cold day in July before she would go out with him. She had tried to talk to him about God, but he wasn't interested. So she just prayed for him.

Patrick and Abigail were quietly talking over by the rose bushes. She knew that Patrick had a great respect for his sister, but thought she was way too uptight about everything in life. She also knew the fondness that Abigail had for her brother. She worried about him constantly and worried about his lifestyle and where it might lead him. She was constantly telling him about God and that he needed to get his life straight. Patrick would just flash her that melting smile of his and tell her that someday he would get his life in order, but right now he was having too much fun to even want to think

# No Regrets

about changing anything.

Sarah could tell, as she watched them talk, that they had started discussing their mother. Their faces had turned somber and serious.

"Patrick," Abigail was saying, "When are you going to grow up? Mother wants you to meet Jesus more than anything. Don't you think you could at least make some effort?"

"I know, sis. I know that's what you have all wanted for me. Believe it or not, I've thought about it a couple of times, even picked up that Bible that you bought me for Christmas and read parts here and there."

"What did you think of what you read?"

"I'm not sure. Sometimes I wish I could believe like you all do, but part of me doesn't want to let go of what is familiar to me in my life."

"Patrick, just please promise me that you won't give up on God. Give Him a chance."

"I won't. I promise to think about it some more. I'm going to go check in on mom now. Want to come with me?"

"That's okay, you go ahead. I'll be in shortly."

Patrick went bounding up the stairs, flashing those gorgeous white teeth Sarah's way and gave her a wink.

There was a hush in the house and Patrick felt as if the sound of his boots on the old hardwood floors were echoing loud enough to be heard even upstairs. Mom had been moved downstairs last month to make it easier on her and on Sarah, as well.

He peeked in the den, where a hospital bed had been put, and noticed his sister, Bailey, was just leaning down to give their mother a kiss on the cheek. When she straightened and turned to leave she saw Patrick standing there, looking, once again, like a lost little boy. She smiled at him, thinking how he tried to act like such a man's man, when really he was still that little boy wondering where his father was and if he would ever come back to him. She gave her brother a hug and told him that their mother was awake and somewhat alert and to enjoy what time he could with her.

Patrick was almost scared to go over to his mother's bed. She looked so fragile, so pale. What if he said something to upset her? His mother spoke his name, beckoning him to come. He realized he had been holding Bailey's hand tightly. She patted his hand and gave him a smile that said everything would be okay. He slowly let go and headed in his mother's direction. He looked back one more time to Bailey for support, but the door was closing.

## Chapter 4

The three women sat out on the porch, two on the swing and one in the wicker chair just on the other side of the door. There they were, three women close in age, a common bond with their belief in God, yet three very different women. They did have another common interest, Patrick. They were all concerned about his lifestyle and his constant pushing away of the Word. This illness that was taking Victoria at such a young age made them all realize just how precious life is and reminded them there were no guarantees of our time here on earth.

"Do you think we could just tie him up somewhere and make him listen?" Bailey suggested in her ever so dramatic way. "What do they call it? An intervention, I believe. Yes, that's it. That's what we should do."

"I don't think you can do an intervention because someone won't believe in God." said Abigail in her all too serious voice, staring off into the unknown.

"I was kidding, Abby." Abby. She hadn't used that name for her sister since they were small. She had always liked it better than Abigail because it didn't sound quite so stiff and old.

"What?" said Abigail, pulling herself back into the present conversation. Had Bailey just called her Abby? Oh, she hoped not. She had always hated when she did that. Abigail was regal and prestigious. She thought it suited her more than Abby.

"Never mind, *Abigail*," said Bailey, rolling her eyes at her sister's never ending seriousness.

"May I make a suggestion?" said Sarah, quietly, half lost in thought. "I suggest that we all get together and pray for Patrick like never before. God said where two or three are gathered together, there shall I be. I say we join our hearts and efforts together for the sake of Patrick's soul."

"Excellent idea, Sarah," said Abigail, Bailey nodding her head in agreement.

"Great," said Sarah. They all stood and joined hands and took turns lifting up Patrick to God. Sarah could feel the fondness and warmth that the two girls had for their brother. She had begun to feel a fondness for him lately, as well. With that done, and promises to do so more throughout the weekend, Sarah headed inside. It was time for Victoria to get another dose of pain killers.

Sarah stood at the door, not wanting to disturb this moment between mother and son. Victoria was quietly talking to her son, her voice just a whisper. Patrick looked like he was trying to understand, wanting to understand the meaning of what she was saying to him. He looked more like a little boy than a man. He looked lost. The harsh reality was that he was lost. He was lost in his sins. As Sarah watched him, she thought she saw a glimpse of recognition on his face. He also looked scared. What was he afraid of? Was it losing his mother or knowing that he was lost. Either way there was a hurt there that only God could heal. The only peace that would come would be from the Father above.

"Oh, God," Sarah whispered, "You promised to be the father of the fatherless. Patrick desperately needs a father right now. Open his eyes to see You are there waiting to hold him in Your arms."

She made a little noise with the door that caused Patrick to jump just a little. She didn't want to interrupt, but she didn't want Victoria in pain either. Patrick looked over at her and motioned for her to come on in.

"Well, Ms. Victoria, are you ready for something to ease the pain I'm sure you're starting to feel?"

Victoria's mouth barely opened as she mouthed a quiet, "Yes." With that Sarah went to work adding more medicine to her IV and checking all of the pumps to make sure they were working properly. She took Victoria's blood pressure and noticed that it had declined. She wondered just how much longer she had. God's timing would be perfect. Sarah believed He would somehow let Victoria hold on until God had set in motion things that would change Victoria's children's lives.

## Chapter 5

Dinner had been prepared and served and all that remained was cleaning off the table and washing the dishes. They all jumped up and joined together in the task at hand. When they finished here they were all going to spend some time with their mother one last time this evening before she retired for the night. Sarah would let them know when their mother had been bathed and changed into a fresh gown for the evening. Sarah was very good about seeing to their mother. She helped her maintain her dignity in her appearance, even as her life slowly slipped away.

They finished their cleaning and waited patiently in the living room. They made small talk, but their thoughts were all on one thing, their mother.

Sarah stepped in from the hallway and told them their mother was ready to see them. She warned them that Victoria was very weak tonight and might not be able to visit for very long. They all glanced at each other and then headed down the hall to what had once been the den.

Bailey was the first to walk in and stopped short,

## No Regrets

almost causing a three person pile up there in the doorway. She was trying so hard to keep her cheery face on, but looking at her mother in such a weak and fragile state made it very hard. How in the world could she laugh her way through this like she had everything else in life?

Abigail, who had stepped on Bailey's heel as she stopped in the doorway, understood the thought that had just flashed on her sister's face. If Bailey couldn't laugh her way through something, she was lost. She gave her sister a reassuring squeeze on her shoulder and gently led her on through the door.

They all three gathered around their mother's bed and just smiled down at her for a few minutes. It seemed like an eternity. Abigail didn't know where it came from, and she didn't recognize her own voice as she almost shouted at her mother, "How can you leave me this responsibility? Why can't you be there for me like a mother should be?"

Horrified, she stepped back and looked as if something or someone else had just spoken through her body. Her mother just looked at her with this look of deep sadness. She looked at her sister, whose wide eyes were mirroring her own. Abigail was shocked at herself and couldn't even utter an apology.

Bailey was next to speak. "How can you say that? She was always there for you. She took care of us and gave us a happy, fun filled home."

The words continued to pour out of Abigail's mouth like a waterfall. "You got the *fun filled life*. You didn't have to take on all the responsibilities that fell on my shoulders while you all were busy having this *fun filled life*. Do you even remember all the times when she was locked in her room? Who do you think wrote out the bills, got the groceries, cooked the meals, got you off to school? It may have been fun for you, but it was very hard for me."

She regretted the words, even as she said them, but they continued to spill out. She didn't dare look at her mother for fear that her words had sent her to her death.

Patrick looked at Abigail with a look of understanding. He had not had to take the responsibilities on that she had, but he knew that their family had been different.

Bailey started to cry as she proclaimed, "No. No, you don't know what you're talking about. Our mother made us laugh and made sure we were taken care of. I don't know what you're talking about." But even as she heard the words she spoke, she knew that there was some truth in what Abigail had spoken. She just chose to remember their childhood differently. She chose to forget the times when their mother was locked behind the doors of her bedroom for days at a time. Chose to forget the times when their mother would make statements about them being better off without her.

Abigail just stood there stunned at her words, and stunned that her younger sister, who had never once talked back to her, was now screaming at her. Did she really see their childhood like that? What was Patrick thinking? She couldn't read his face. She couldn't tell if it was disbelief, sadness, understanding, or empathy. What did this boy that she had practically raised think of her now after her outburst.

"Oh, mother," Abigail wailed, "I'm so sorry. I didn't mean those words. I'm just so overwhelmed by all of this. Please, forgive me. I didn't mean it. I love you so much." She was kneeled down beside the bed weeping for the words she knew had hurt her family, for the loss of her childhood, for so many things that had been bottled up inside of her for so long.

Bailey and Patrick just stood there, wide eyed, not knowing what to do. They looked at their mother, pleading for her to not be hurt by what had just happened. How could they ever make this right?

Victoria placed her boney hand that had skin as thin as parchment paper, upon Abigail's head. She patted her daughter's head and whispered, "It's okay. I understand, and someday I pray you will, too."

Sarah stepped up to the bed and said, "Ms. Victoria, it's time." Victoria looked at her with fear in her eyes. The children looked at each other wondering what it was time for. Sarah continued, "Your mother has lived a life that was just as confusing to her as it was to you. She has been telling me her story to write down for you to read after she passes, but I think now is the time." Victoria gave her an approving nod and closed her eyes to rest.

## Chapter 6

The children quietly left and gathered back in the living room. They were all left dazed and confused, not knowing how they felt about anything, wondering what they were about to hear. What could their mother possibly say to them about their childhood? Had she been on drugs? Did she have a secret life? The mind can think of a thousand things when left to itself for even a few minutes.

Sarah entered carrying a spiral notebook. It was obvious by the worn and tattered cover that it had been used quite a bit. Sarah sat down in the Queen Anne chair that their mother had loved to sit in and read in the afternoons. She could see the garden from this window, which always relaxed her and made her smile.

Sarah looked at each one of them slowly, a look of love on her face. In the short fourteen months that she had been taking care of Victoria she had come to love each one of them as family. She did not consider herself just a caretaker to Victoria, but to all of them. She took a deep breath and let it out slowly. "Would it be okay if I prayed before we continued?" Everyone nodded a yes, still shocked and bewildered at the past events of the last hour. Sarah prayed, "Father, I come to You right now asking that You pour down Your peace on this household. Lord, You are the only One that can bring understanding and healing to each heart. Open their hearts and their ears and their eyes to the story of another child of Yours, Ms. Victoria. You've brought healing and understanding to her life and now it's her prayer that You do the same for her children. I thank You, Lord, for Your kindness and mercy and grace. Amen."

Everyone looked a little more relaxed, but still confused and waiting in anticipation. Sarah moved her eyes from one person to another as she explained that Victoria had asked her to write down parts about her life that they hadn't known about or, along with her, had not understood.

Sarah opened the tattered notebook and began to read.

# Chapter 7

My dearest children, I'm not exactly sure why I am writing this to you, but felt I must. I cannot stand the thought of leaving this earth without at least trying to get you to understand just how much I loved you. I offer no excuses for not being the best mother. I often wondered why God had entrusted me with three children that I felt inadequate to raise, but I know that He has special plans for you and that I was just blessed enough to be with you while He led you down the paths that are leading you to those plans.

You will probably ask why I didn't share this with you earlier, but the truth is, I'm not sure why I didn't. Perhaps I still felt some shame or didn't want you to feel ashamed of me. I'm not sure. Maybe it was selfish of me to withhold this part of my life from you, but please know I only did the best I could. There are parts that I don't feel like I should go into detail, but they are so much a part of my life that they need be mentioned.

Lord, please guide my words, because I surely don't know where to begin. I might as well start at the beginning and work my way through.

# No Regrets

*You know your grandmother and grandfather were strong Christians. They showed us plenty of love and led a life that led me to Christ. So what horrible thing could come from a home like that? Well, it wasn't our home that brought evil into my life, it was the home of a relative.*

*I loved my relatives, I won't say which relatives I'll be speaking of because I do not want you to harbor bad feelings towards them. I loved them then and even though they caused me much pain throughout my life, I love them now. I've learned to not only forgive them, but after many years, to forget the evil and search out the good. There's no easy way to say this, but I was molested all during my childhood. I did not even remember the majority of this abuse until later on in life, but in my body and mind I knew it and it affected me in ways that I never understood until much later. There was one time that stood out in my mind every day of my life. It was the very last time.*

*I was thirteen and had just lost one of my best friends to leukemia. Everyone thought it would be good for me to get away for a while, and I was okay with that. I would come back for the funeral and then return to my relative's house. That morning was the day that changed my life forever. I'm not sure what was different about that time, except to say that I felt like my friend's day of mourning was violated. That day has played in my head almost every single day since then. It was a couple of years before I even told partially what had happened to me. Those two years were filled with other relative's deaths, medical problems, you name it. My teen years were filled with secret desires to die. Of course, this wasn't exactly something I could share, so I held it all in. I was good at holding things in, stuffing them down into the recess of my conscious.*

*They say that burying all of that within myself threw my*

## Michele Murry

system all out of kilter. Once those chemicals in my brain became imbalanced, there was no reversing that. During that day and age we didn't have anyone who knew about such things, so it went undiagnosed.

From there it was a series of things. While still in high school I had to have a lump removed from my breast, which was a very scary thing to go through, but once again I smiled and laughed my way through. I lost a number of friends, married Abigail's father, who, even though he was a dear friend, was not someone that I was in love with. When he was killed I was shattered. How was I supposed to raise this baby all by myself? I really didn't have the confidence in myself to be able to handle the responsibility.

I tried to kill myself shortly after his death. I didn't feel worthy of having this precious child. I didn't want to ruin her life. I didn't want to have to keep facing tragedy after tragedy. I just didn't have the strength to carry on. I know that some may have looked at that as selfish and horrible, but in my mind you would've been raised by normal people, Abigail. I sure didn't feel normal at this stage of my life.

I was so depressed most of the time that I could barely work and come home and take care of a child. I wanted to, desperately. I looked at my friends and the energy they had with their children and all the things they did with them, but I couldn't muster up the strength or the knowledge of how to do that.

With each passing year I felt more abnormal than normal. I tried to talk to a few friends about it. I didn't know what was wrong, but I knew that I wasn't like everyone else. I just wanted to feel normal. But everyone kept telling me that I was normal. If they only knew.

My thoughts were obsessed with dying. I would make plans of how I could die and make it look accidental, so not

## No Regrets

to shame my family. I tried to plan times for my death so that you would be with people that loved you and could take care of you. I knew these thoughts were not normal, but I didn't know what I could do to convince someone that there was something wrong. So I just lived in my strange little world.

The men flowed in and out of my life. I wanted to be loved as much as I wanted to be normal. Somehow I had gotten the misconception that the only way a man would love me is by what I could do for him, or with my body. I now see how that tied into my abuse. I was taught early that sex was love. A very sick and demented lie, but that's what I was shown from a very early age, so I somehow believed it.

## Chapter 8

Victoria tried to sleep, but it was hard, knowing that she was being laid bare and her life exposed to her children. She knew that she had nothing to be ashamed of. She had gone over that in her mind a million times, but the pain was still raw after all these years.

It wasn't her own shame that bothered her. What if her children were ashamed of her? What if they saw her disease as something shameful? It was almost better to have them think she was irresponsible all these years rather than crazy. Would they think she was crazy?

A tear ran out of the corner of her eye and dropped with a thud to her pillow. She loved those three more than anyone could ever possibly understand. She couldn't stand it if they looked upon her in shame now. Maybe she was wrong to have told them. She didn't know anymore. But leaving, knowing that her children were in pain over the childhood that she had given them, she couldn't bear that either.

She closed her eyes as the tears continued to hit her pillow like the thick heavy raindrops of a Texas summer. "God, You've carried me all these years. You've kept me

## No Regrets

close to Your side when I thought I was all alone. God, I'm tired and weak. I want to come home, but please grant me this last request. Please help my children to understand how much I loved them. Let them understand that even through times of our lives when we think there is no point to our living, that You still have Your hand on us, guiding us to where we can fulfill Your plans for our lives. I want them to be able to look back on our lives together and smile. Thank You, Lord, for bringing me this far. I can't wait to see Your face."

The look of peace was on her face as she fell back into a state of sleep. The tears had stopped and dried a thin trail of salt on her face.

## Chapter 9

Abigail and Bailey went to get everyone something to drink. They talked in hushed tones as they wondered what the rest of their mother's life had entailed. They could have never guessed that her young life had started out so painfully. She was a devout Christian, came from a Christian home. It was all so hard to absorb.

Once everyone had something cold to drink, they all settled back down in their seats and gave Sarah their full attention. There were so many questions that they wanted to ask, but Sarah had asked them to let her read through to the end before discussing any of it.

"Let's see, where did we leave off," Sarah said looking over the page. "Oh, yes, here we are." She sat her glass of tea down and glanced back down at the notebook that held the secrets of Victoria's life.

*After a few years of dragging you, Abigail, from place to place, seeking the love I so hungrily desired, I met Bailey's father, Troy. I was so thrilled to be noticed by someone of his prestige. Why would someone of his social stature even take a second glance at me? I was thrilled, certain that my life* was about to change and be normal.

He was good to Abigail and didn't mind buying me things. He had a number of indiscretions, but I just figured that it was somehow my fault, I wasn't good enough in some way, so I overlooked them. I just knew that when I had his baby I would be good enough and he wouldn't stray anymore.

He loved you girls. He was so proud of you. He would have me buy you all kinds of fancy little dresses and parade you around the bank when we would go meet him for lunch. I would also notice the look between him and a few of the tellers, but surely I was good enough for him now. I was the mother of his child.

The indiscretions became so bad that he even got an apartment in town and stayed there several nights out of the week. I knew that I may not be worth much, but I was worth more than that, so we left.

I'm sorry Bailey, I didn't want you to know about that. Please know that I forgave him and we were able to become somewhat friends after a while.

During this time I had also began the endless circle of jobs. I knew I was smart and could do anything I wanted, so I did. I would get my insurance license and be so excited about finally having a career, but soon the depression would kick back in and I would slowly lose interest until that job was finally played out. I kept thinking that maybe if I had a career, was important, that I could finally be happy, satisfied. But career after career just made me feel worse because I couldn't stick with any one thing. What was wrong with me? Other people chose a career and stuck with it, why couldn't I?

## Chapter 10

Bailey had to leave the room for a minute to catch her breath. She had heard rumors about her father, but to hear it from her mother and think about the affects it had on her, that was a different story altogether.

She walked out onto the back deck. The weather was absolutely perfect for an early Spring night. There was a slight breeze blowing that raised the hair up on her arms, but it felt good. She breathed in that clean crisp air that she didn't have the privilege of in the city. She also didn't get to see the million stars that were shining bright tonight back in the city. She realized how much she loved it here. She had always thought of herself as a city girl, like her father, but now she realized that she missed the simpleness of country living.

Her mother always dreamed of moving to the country, to simplify life, she would say. Standing there, Bailey finally understood what she meant by that. Right now she would give anything for a simple, stress free life. Would she ever have that?

Somehow she felt like some prize or trophy that her

father had used her mother to get. She would have to spend some time with God trying to figure out how she felt about that.

She was trying to keep her head about all of this. It was so much to absorb at once. How had her mom managed to smile and laugh so much through the years. No wonder she spent days at a time locked behind her bedroom door.

There was still so much she didn't understand about her mother's behavior through the years, but she was realizing something, her mother had painted on a smile and laughed when on the inside she was barely hanging on.

How could someone have so many false beliefs about themselves and life and be so close to God at the same time? Why did God allow her to go through all that she had? Why couldn't she live longer now that she seemingly had come to terms with her past and to some sort of understanding with God? There was so many questions, so many mixed feelings rolling around in her head. She wanted to go running in to be with her mother, talk to her, ask her questions, but she knew that she needed the rest of the story first.

Did she even have a right to ask her mother questions about her past? That was another thing she would have to discuss with God. Her mother was on the brink of death. Somehow it seemed selfish to want answers that she might not even be entitled to. Bailey felt as if the words she was hearing in there were sacred. It was almost like reading her diary. She would've felt guilty had her mother not initiated their gaining this knowledge.

Patrick closed the sliding glass door and walked over to where she was standing. "Wow," he said, "I had forgotten what a Spring night in the country was like." He put his arm around her protectively. "Are you okay, sis?"

She looked down, picking at her fingernail, trying to figure out if she was or not. Patrick just stood by her quietly, patiently.

"Yes," she replied after a few moments, "If mother could manage to live out what we're hearing, then I am certainly going to be okay hearing it, right?"

Patrick grinned down at his sister. When had he gotten so much taller than her? He could see the top of her blonde head. He led her back to the living room and everyone got settled back in to hear the rest of their mother's story.

# Chapter 11

As Sarah looked down at the pages she had been reading, she wondered if these three people truly understood the depth of what Victoria was trying to tell them. She was only covering the surface of what had been a grueling life. Did they understand what it had been like for her going through life with a mental disorder and trying to live normal and make a normal life for them? She wondered if they had even begun to realize that their mother was describing to them her mental state. Were they seeing beyond the surface? Surely they didn't just see the situation as that of someone who hasn't gotten their life together.

To live with a mental disorder was hard enough, but Victoria hadn't even been aware that there was something truly wrong. She knew something didn't click, but everyone just kept telling her she was normal, so she tried to live like it the best way she knew how, one day at a time with God.

Everyone was once again settled in their seats and ready for Sarah to continue. Sarah looked at each one of them, saying a silent prayer that God would let them see

## Michele Murry

what their mother was really trying to say to them. Then she looked back down to where she had left off.

*I met your father, Patrick, shortly after separating from Troy. I had married my best friend, that hadn't worked out. I had married a successful banker, that hadn't worked out. Now I had met Bruce, a man as burly as his name. I thought maybe this was what I needed, someone who wasn't so concerned with money, who was just a normal guy.*

*It was only a short time after our meeting that I learned I was pregnant. I was thrilled. Finally, we could settle down and have a normal family. But our family was far from normal. I no sooner found out I was pregnant that I also found out Bruce was a drug addict and alcoholic. A couple of times he told me he would try to quit, but it never lasted more than a day.*

*I had hoped that our having a baby would give him the incentive he needed to quit once and for all, but it didn't. He did love you, I want you to know that. He knew that he was not good father material, so his way of loving you was not exposing you to that kind of life.*

*So here I am, with three precious children, barely able to take care of myself each day. I had no idea how I would raise you, but I had no other choice than to trust God to raise you. I prayed for you everyday. I felt so inadequate to have children. I didn't know how to make a steady living, even though I could do just about anything. I couldn't give you my full attention because I could barely make it through the stresses of life. Most of the time I wanted to die, continued planning my death almost daily. I would shut down for days at a time and lock myself away in my bedroom so you wouldn't have to see me that way.*

*During those times I would cry out to God to either make me normal or let me die. I knew what a burden I was to you, Abigail. You shouldn't have had to take care of the others and especially me. I was the mother. I was supposed to take care of you. The strain showed in your eyes even though you never complained. My heart hurt so bad every time I would look at those eyes that were way too grown up for your tender age. It broke my heart.*

*I loved God with all my heart, tried my best to live a life that would please Him, but it seemed all I could do was fail. I was certain that even though I worked hard for Him, I wasn't worthy of His blessings. Look how I had twisted my life all around into distorted knots. I saw only a life filled with failures.*

*I had tried every class of man and still no one would love me. You can't imagine how empty I felt, how great my desire for love was. Wasn't there anyone out there that could love me for who I was?*

*I didn't even know how to fake my way through life anymore. It wasn't working. I was spiraling down into an abyss.*

*Thirteen years ago I hit rock bottom. I didn't know what else to do. I had never been involved with drugs or alcohol, but for some reason I felt like an addict who had hit the bottom of the barrel.*

*I got to the point where I couldn't eat, couldn't sleep. I was so dehydrated I couldn't even move off of the couch. I told you three that I had the flu, but the truth was I was dying. My pain was finally killing me. I had lost the will to live and had just given up.*

*You, my dear Abigail, were only seventeen years old then and had the weight of the world upon your shoulders worrying about me while taking care of the others. You were scared to go to school. I could see the pain in your eyes. You were afraid if you left, I'd die there by myself. You contin-*

ued on, though, with a strength that I wish I could've experienced.

One day while you all were at school I had come to the end. I had tried to die many times, wished for it, begged for it, but the time was here. I got every pill that the doctors had prescribed for me and I poured them all out in the kitchen floor where I sat. I got me a glass of water and determined that this was the end.

As I gathered up the pills I realized something, I didn't really want to die. I wanted to live, but I wanted to live a normal life. I called your grandfather and sobbed into the phone my desire to live. He didn't understand at first, but understanding soon began to come to light.

At the time I thought that was the worse day of my life, but to be honest, it was the beginning of a whole new life for me. We moved here so that I could be close to family, let someone help me. I had been too proud to ask for help before, didn't really know how to, or what to ask for. But I had no more pride to lose, it was time to make some changes, no matter what that entailed.

I hated moving you kids again. I had moved you almost once a year all of your life, but I had no choice. We wouldn't make it out there on our own any longer.

Sarah needed to check on Victoria. She placed the book on the side table and excused herself.

## Chapter 12

Sarah tiptoed into the room, not wanting to wake Victoria. She administered more medicine to the IV and made sure everything was working as it should. She placed her hand on Victoria's hand, noticing how much colder it was than before.

Victoria stirred and looked up at Sarah with so many questions in her eyes. "It's okay, Ms. Victoria," Sarah assured her, "God is in control. You've raised three wonderful children. I can tell how much they love you and share your pain as I read to them. Quit your worrying. You lived your life to the best of your ability. God will honor your request in this matter."

"I sure hope you're right, Sarah. I feel like I've hurt them more than enough in my lifetime, I don't want to hurt them anymore."

"You let God worry about how your life's testimony is used. You've helped so many because of the life you went through."

"You're right. I know this. I guess I'm just still trying to take control of the situation every once in a while." Victoria lay there quietly for a minute and her chin begin to quiver. "Do you think they'll think I am a nutcase?"

Sarah let out a hardy laugh. "Ms. Victoria, we're all nutcases in this world. Any sane person would have to be to make it through the evil that runs rampant on this earth nowadays. Is that what you're most worried about?"

"I can't help it." The tears were running freely down the sides of her face again. "I know I am *different*, but I'm not a nut. How could I stand to look at my children again if I knew they thought that?"

"Ms. Victoria, if you're a nutcase then you're the sanest nutcase I've ever known. Bi-polar is a medical condition. How many times have your doctors told you it's not any different than having something like diabetes? You went through some horrible traumas when you were young. When you weren't able to express them or deal with them properly your chemicals got a little out of whack. You take medicine to keep them somewhat in line. You know that doesn't constitute you being a nut. The fact that you've gotten this far in life, raised three children and survived all of Satan's attacks to take your life is amazing. If anything, your children should be very proud that you were able to survive. You could've succumbed to the urges of suicide long ago. You could've abandoned your children. You could've turned to drugs and alcohol like most bi-polar people do, but you didn't. You stuck close to God as He allowed you to go through the things you've experienced and you have a wonderful testimony because of it. Now, wipe those tears. I need to go finish telling your children how brave and strong you were."

She leaned down and gave Victoria a kiss on the

cheek and patted her hand. How she loved this dear woman of God. She prayed a quick prayer of comfort as she left the room and chuckled to herself. "A nutcase. Of all the crazy people in the world she thinks *she's* a nutcase?"

Sarah walked back into the living room, noticing that it was very quiet. What were they thinking? She was certain she saw love and compassion in their eyes. It would be interesting to talk to them after she finished.

"How's mother doing?" asked Abigail.

"She's resting as best she can. Are you ready to hear the rest of her story?"

## Chapter 13

Sarah could see the questions arising in their eyes. She thought they looked tired, like they had gone on a long journey. They had.

When we first moved close to your grandparents, I was just so relieved to feel like I wasn't alone anymore. That feeling of loneliness was enough to sling me to the end of my rope. Hopefully this time would be different. We could have a stable, steady life. This was country living, plain and simple.

There were still many things to sort through, decisions to make. I could tell my parents didn't really know what to do with me. Join the crowd, I didn't either. At least someone knew how I felt now, that was a huge weight lifted off of my shoulders.

It wasn't long before my father had set me up with a counselor. We all knew I needed some kind of help, we just weren't sure what. This was a start.

It wasn't far into our visits that my counselor began to see patterns and parts of my life that led him to believe that I was bi-polar. I hate that word. It sounds so, oh, I don't know, mental. However, I was anxious to find out if I truly was. At least I would have a name, an explanation as to *why I had always felt different.*

*A few trips to other doctors confirmed what we suspected. I don't think I had ever been happier over being diagnosed with a disease. You have to understand, I spent almost all of my life feeling different and not understanding why. It was enough to drive a person crazy.*

*I'll let Sarah explain to you exactly what bi-polar is. She's much better at that.*

"Would you like for me to explain that now or wait?" Sarah said, looking questioningly at them.

Patrick raised his hand as he spoke up, almost looking like a school boy asking the teacher a question. "I'd appreciate it if you would explain it now. I've never heard of it."

"Bi-polar is a mental condition that has to do with the chemicals in your brain. It usually comes about when a person experiences some great trauma, but doesn't deal properly with their emotions. In your mother's case, her molestation was the main trigger. Once the chemicals in the brain are imbalanced, they can never just go back to being balanced. Your mother takes medications to help keep them as balanced as possible, but she still has to monitor her moods. When a person is bi-polar their moods swing from extremely high to extremely low and back to extremely high. Where we have bad days and really good days, your mother's moods go from being very depressed for a period, and then overly up for an amount of time. You may have noticed that after her periods of staying in her room she might go to the extreme of being happy all of the sudden."

"Is that the same as manic-depressive?" asked Bailey.

"Yes, manic-depressive is another name that the

condition is often called. The best way I can explain it is to compare it to diabetes. A diabetic has an imbalance in their body. They take insulin to help keep their blood sugar level in check. Just because they are using insulin or dieting properly doesn't mean that they don't have diabetes anymore or that they won't have any problems with their blood sugar level, it just means that they have to take medicine that helps them live as normal a life as possible. Your mother has lived all these years with this condition and no medications to help keep her balanced. The fact that she has gone this many years and led even a half-way normal, productive life is amazing. The strength it must've taken to hang on like she did is unbelievable."

They all three sat there trying to absorb this new information. It kind of shed a whole new light on their mother. She was going from irresponsible mother, to hero mother quickly, but the realization that they were receiving this information when it was too late to treat her as the hero they were learning she was, was almost disheartening. They sat staring at Sarah, waiting to find out about this character in a story, that just happened to be their mother.

*I was so thankful to have a name for this disease that had all but ruined my life. I did whatever the doctors told me to in order to get it under control. The prospect of feeling normal for the first time was unbelievable. It was also scary. It was new territory for me. I had never felt normal that I could ever remember. What would people expect of me if I was finally normal? What if I couldn't succeed at being normal? I know those seem like silly things to worry about, but I was all of the sudden being thrown into a world that I had no knowledge of. Still, I pressed on, determined to at*

# No Regrets

*least give normal a try.*

*I saw doctors and therapists weekly for over two years. I tried to tell you about it and where I was going a million times, but the words could never form. I was afraid that you would think I had gone crazy or that other kids would tease you if they found out, so I kept it to myself.*

*Finally, by the time I was leading a somewhat normal life, you were all almost grown. I felt so bad that I hadn't been able to go back and be the mom that I had wanted to be. I thanked God every single day for watching over us all and for raising you, Himself.*

*I don't have bad feelings about being bi-polar, and all the little disorders that I had developed along with it; anxiety disorders, agoraphobia, panic attacks. In fact, I knew I had to reach out to others that might be experiencing what I had for so many years. I still didn't feel usable by God, but I continued to pray faithfully that He would use me in whatever way He could.*

*He has. When He finally got me to realize how much He truly loves me, what real love is, then He used me in ways I never thought possible. I've had the opportunity to work with abused women and children at the shelters. I've been used to help women and young girls figure out what true love is. I've been able to speak to groups I never thought possible, sing at places I've only dreamed of in times past.*

*I realize that God was preparing me. The things that He allowed me to go through were not meant to hurt me. Satan may have sought to take my life, but God had me under the protection of His wing the whole time, grooming me, growing my faith, so that I could be an effective witness for Him.*

*I made so many mistakes along the way, but I have no regrets. Had I not gone through those times, I never could've been used by God the way I was.*

# Chapter 14

Sarah, paused, letting the words sink in. They thought they had known their mother so well, but they were learning that they knew very little about her.

"So when mother would be gone all day once a week, it was doctors she was going to see instead of some fantasy man I had imagined?" Bailey said, her head cocked to one side.

Patrick let out a bellow, "You definitely have mom's sense of humor. How can you two find something funny in every single situation?"

"I guessed I learned to laugh instead of cry, like she did. But I don't want to hold it all inside. Can I get this disease, this condition?"

"It is genetic," Sarah said, "but I don't think just having her sense of humor makes you bi-polar."

Abigail rolled her eyes. "You always have to be so dramatic, Bailey."

"Hey, at least I know how to laugh."

"What are you saying? Are you saying that I don't ever laugh? I was too busy to laugh."

"Whoa! Now girls, let's not get all excited." Patrick said, his tone of voice patronizing, which led to the girls giving him a look that told him to watch it.

Sarah stepped in and saved him from the wrath of his sisters. "Okay, let's not get off track. We don't have the time to waste on petty arguments." She had put a look of shame and guilt on all of their faces, which hadn't been her intention, but seemed almost humorous the way they all did it in sync.

"Do you think we might could see mother again tonight," Abigail asked.

"I'll see how she's feeling when we've finished. I still have a little bit more to read to you."

"Oh, I'm sorry, Sarah, I thought you were finished."

"Almost, just a small personal note for each of you."

## Chapter 15

They looked at each other, wondering what their mother would say to each of them. Sarah took a drink of her tea that was quickly turning to water, dripping some of the sweat from the glass onto the notebook. She quickly reached and blotted the water with her sleeve, thankful the words had not smeared.

*To my darling Abigail,*

*You have always amazed me with your maturity. I suppose you didn't have much choice in the matter, but I respect you and am so proud of you. You have grown into a successful young woman. I ask one thing of you, learn to be a child again. A lot of your childhood was taken from you, and for that I am so very sorry, but it's never too late to let the child in you emerge. Take long walks and pick the flowers. Laugh and giggle with your sister until your cheeks hurt. Lay in the grass on a summer day and let your imagination turn the clouds into animals. God said that we are to come to Him as a child. Let Him hold you in His lap like the father you never knew. He will, you know. He still lets me climb*

## No Regrets

*into His lap and lay my head on His bosom. You know how much I always loved the song,* **I Hope You Dance***, by LeeAnn Womack. Listen to it again. It is my wish for you.*

Sarah paused to look up at Abigail. There was a transformation in her face. It was as if she finally had permission to be a child.

*My precious Bailey,*

*Always a sparkle in my day. I love the way you don't let society govern the way you should dress or act. Good for you. The ability to laugh in even the most serious of situations will keep your spirit healthy. Laughter is like good medicine for the heart. Even God agrees with you on that. For you, my dynamic one, I wish balance. What do I mean by that? Well, I want laughter to be a part of your daily life, but don't forget that it is okay to cry sometimes too. Allow yourself to hurt. Just be true to your emotions. Never cover them up. They will eventually eat at your heart, making it numb. You are full of compassion and energy. You can't have compassion if you become numb.*

The tears flowed freely down Bailey's cheeks. How did her mom know her so well? She was afraid of the compassion that welled up inside of her. She had learned that you get hurt when you care too much. But she would try. She was learning that this woman that she had looked at as being totally carefree, was also very wise. She had always wanted to be like her mom when it came to having fun. Now she wanted to be like her in all ways.

## Michele Murry

Dear Patrick, my precious baby boy,

    *I have so many wishes for you. I wish you could forgive your father. I wish you could realize the world cannot fill that void in your heart. I wish you could let yourself be loved, not keep yourself separate from those that love you. You can be anything you want to be, go as far as you want, just please remember that nothing is worth having without God. It can make you happy for a while, but when the glitter fades it's just another thing. Patrick, please don't shut God out completely. Give Him a chance to show you how much He loves you. He promises to be a father to the fatherless. Let Him. I want to have the assurance that I will see you again someday. I want you to join me in heaven when your life is finished. There's only one way to do that. No one can make the decision of giving your heart and life to Christ except you, but never be afraid to reach out to others to help you find your way there. Ask God to make things clear to you. Ask Him to reveal Himself to you. He will. Read Luke in your Bible, and be receptive to what God has to say to you. I love you, baby boy. Never forget that.*

    Patrick looked as though he might bolt from the room. Sarah wasn't sure what it was she was seeing in his eyes. It looked like a mixture of confusion, thankfulness, and fear. He did end up bolting. They heard the screen door slam shut where he had burst through it. The three girls looked at each other with the same question playing on their lips.
    Sarah finally broke the silence, "Let's let him have some time to himself."
    The two sisters nodded their heads like robots. They finally started asking Sarah questions about their

mother. It was like she was a whole different person to them now. They were still sorting through their emotions stemming from what they had heard tonight, but they were fascinated with this woman that laid in there just a couple of doors away, waiting for God's angels to come and take her away.

Sarah finally left them to go check on Victoria. The girls really wanted to see her one last time before retiring to bed.

The two girls sat there alone in the room. For the first time ever there was an awkwardness. They were at ease with each other, they just weren't sure what they were suppose to say right then. Abigail finally took her sister's hand and said, "Let's pray and then go find Patrick."

The two sisters got on their knees with their hands joined, leaning on the edge of the couch. They hadn't prayed together like this in years. Things were going to change, though. It was time for them to unite together and be the sisters they had once been. The beginning of change took place right there in their mother's living room floor, as they poured out their hearts in one accord for their brother, Patrick.

## Chapter 16

The girls were still sitting in the floor when Patrick came back in. He could hear the laughter as soon as he opened the front door. He didn't know whether to laugh with them or to be mad at them for laughing as they waited for their mother to die.

He slid in the door and had a seat across the room from them in his favorite overstuffed chair. They were still on their knees in front of the couch, so they didn't see him come in. How could they be so happy during such a sad time. He decided he would ask them just that as soon as they stopped their giggle session.

Another couple of minutes passed and the girls were able to control their laughter, wiping tears from their face. When had Patrick come in? Why hadn't he said anything?

"Hey, Patrick," Abigail said as she took a Kleenex from the box on the side table and blew her nose. "Are you okay?"

"Yes, and I see you two seem to be just fine." He still wasn't sure if he was hurt or mad or jealous.

"What's wrong, Patrick? Would you like to talk?"

# No Regrets

Bailey never was one to hesitate with her questions.

"Yes. No. I don't know. I'm not sure about anything right now."

"Would you like to ask us some questions about God?" Abigail said.

"I don't think I can right now, sis. My mind is so jumbled. I don't think I was ever meant to take in this much information at one time." He finally couldn't resist throwing a little grin their way. At least he knew they loved him.

Bailey got up from her place on the floor and walked over to her younger brother, plopping right down in his lap, causing him to grunt. She hugged him as tightly as she could and said, "Patrick, we love you and we are always here for you. We have the same wish for you that mother does. Please come talk to us when you're ready." With that she jumped up, gave her a sister a warm smile that hadn't been there earlier and said she was going to the kitchen for hot chocolate if anyone was interested. Abigail followed, giving Patrick a peck on the cheek as she passed.

Patrick stayed where he was, he needed some time to think. He reached for the Bible that his mother kept on her coffee table. What was the book she had asked him to read, Luke? He opened up the Bible and searched until he found the right book. All those words looked so foreign to him, jumbled on the page. He started to close the book and return it to its proper place, but stopped and opened it again.

"God, I'm not sure how I'm suppose to talk to You. I see this relationship that my mother and my sisters have with You and I honestly don't understand it. I'm not even sure, yet, if I want to understand it. But if You know me at all, then You know that the lady laying in that bed in there is the most important woman in my life. She may not have been perfect, but she's the only parent I've ever had. I don't know what she means by You being my Father. All I know is that I love her, and I don't want to go to a different place than her when I die. If You're real, please show me."

He started with chapter one and got to chapter three when he heard Sarah coming down the hall. He marked his place. He wasn't sure if he understood what he was reading, but he was finding it interesting.

## Chapter 17

Sarah led the three young adults down the hall to their mother's room, but didn't join them as they entered. This was a time for family and she knew when she needed to stand back. Her place now was to find a quiet place to spend a little time in prayer concerning this family.

In some ways Victoria's fears sounded petty to her. She had an illness. Yes, it had affected her life and even the lives of her children, but it was an illness for goodness sake. There are some things we have no control over in this life.

Sarah thought she understood what really bothered Victoria about it all. She knew Victoria had a love for her children like every mother did, so whether or not Victoria had control over the situations of the past, they still haunted her. She still carried a certain amount of shame and guilt for things that were not her burdens to carry. How can someone of such faith still hang on to things that should be left at the foot of the cross?

I guess no matter how mature you are in life or in your Christian walk, there are always lessons to be learned. Victoria needed to learn some things about herself and come to terms with her past as much as her children.

Sarah found her way to the sunroom, which was off of the kitchen. There was no sun shining through at this time of night, but there was a full moon that lit up the entire room. She didn't bother to turn on the light. She wanted to embrace the darkness. It made her feel as if she were being hugged and held tight to God's bosom, with the only light being that which radiated from His heart.

This had been her favorite spot over the last several months. Each night, after she had seen to Victoria one last time, she would come here and sit in the wicker rocking chair that sat facing the back windows. She would stare at the moon and rock slowly, talking to God.

People didn't understand that this job was not exactly easy on her. Her job was to take care of people at the end of their lives and to help lead them safely over to the other side. Sometimes she would get patients that weren't Christians. They would break her heart when they would refuse to listen as she tried to tell them how much God loved them. She tried to remember that it was her job to go where God led and do what He told her. They were responsible for their response. It didn't make losing someone she had become fond of to spend eternity in hell any easier. Each family lost someone dear to them, but she did, too.

This family made her smile. They were a hodgepodge of sorts. Victoria was almost like one of the children. She was strong and faithful to God, but even after all she had gone through in her life she had this sense of innocence about her. It only took one look in her eyes to know that her innocence in this world had been shattered many years ago, but she had a childlike faith and trust that made you want to draw her close to you and tell her how special she is. She knew God loved her, but I think she could stand to have her worth reiterated each and every day. I honestly think she missed the look her children gave her when they talked to her. There was a respect there, a depth of love that had not been shattered by their strange upbringing.

Those three. She loved them like her own siblings. Another downfall of this job. When the job was over, they would be gone, also. They would walk away closer to each other, and she would walk away alone.

They may have wondered about their life growing up, even sometimes resenting that their mother was not like other mother's, but nothing had ever diminished their love for her. I think they were not only having to deal with the information that explained so much of their childhood, but maybe a spark of guilt, too. After all, they had made remarks over the years that they knew had hurt their mother, even as recently as today. They were wondering, as much as their mother was, if they had lost a bit of love because of their actions.

"God, how can your children be so blind to Your unconditional love? Will they ever see that their worth is not based on their actions, but who they are through Your Son's sacrifice? Here they are, battling with their own private pains, when there are others right in front of them that want to be there for them. My time is almost over here, Lord. Have I shone Your love on them in the way that You meant for me to? Patrick still hasn't come around, yet, God. Is there something else that I need to do or say or show him that will help him find His way to

You? I just pray that You heal each person in this family. Help them to forgive the past, acknowledge their worth, and point their futures towards You. Give me wisdom in making their lives a little easier as Ms. Victoria goes home to You. Amen."

She sat there for a while longer, humming the church hymns that brought her so much comfort in times like these.

## Chapter 18

At first they just stood around her bed, listening to the sound of the pump. Their mother looked as if she was sleeping, and they weren't sure if they should have disturbed her tonight or not.

With eyes still closed Victoria whispered, "Sit."

They pulled up their chairs to her bed and Abigail reached out and took her hand. Her hand was so frail now, that she was almost afraid to touch it, but she did, gently laying her hand on top of her mother's.

The silence continued for another few minutes, seeming like an eternity. Bailey was the first to speak up. "Mother, I want you to know that my respect has grown for you. I used to think that you were just not cut out to be a mother, but now that I have more information, I know that it not only took great courage and strength to raise three kids and keep yourself from going under, but you also did it blind sided. You didn't know what you were up against. It's hard to fight what you cannot see."

The dam broke behind Abigail's eyes and she leaned her head against the side of the bed, letting her body shake with sobs. No one moved. They let her empty her emotions until they subsided. Abigail was so embarrassed. She was the strong one, the one who never cried or showed emotions. She had cried like a baby in the past twenty-four hours and she wasn't used to that. She felt shame and guilt. She had always associated tears with weakness, and she had worked her whole life to portray strength. She felt her cheeks turn crimson red as she realized that all eyes were on her.

Her mother's words had a gentleness to them that did not berate or judge. "Abigail, please tell me what the rivers you have cried today have been for."

Abigail squirmed in her chair, finding no comfortable position. Could she put into words what her tears were for? She wasn't sure, but her mother had challenged her to let herself feel emotions, and she would do her best to share them now, as she tried to understand them herself.

"If I say I don't know, will it be someone else's turn?" The corners of her mouth turned up into a grin as she looked over at her brother and sister. Bailey feigned horror in her overly dramatic way, but her eyes told her sister that she would be here for her as she explored this new territory.

Abigail reached for a Kleenex and wiped her eyes and blew her nose. She reached for another, sensing that she would probably need it shortly. "I don't know, Mother. There are so many things that are heavy on my heart. Everything seems so...so emotional right now. You know how uncomfortable I am with that." She looked at her mother hoping that her short explanation would suffice, but all eyes continued to stare at her silently, waiting for her to go on. "I feel guilt, loads of guilt. I have always loved you and Bailey and Patrick, but I resented the role that I was forced to play in our family." She dropped her eyes, not willing to see if they were seeing down into the depths of her soul and seeing just how far the resentment had gone over the years. Her chin quivered. She played with the Kleenex in her hand, took a deep breath, and continued. "Mother, I always thought you were irresponsible and selfish. I thought you didn't want us, and so had no desire to take care of us. I resented Bailey and Patrick for being allowed to have their childhood. They enjoyed the fun times, watched cartoons, and played with their friends during the bad times, while I took care of everything." The sobs were starting to return and she cried into her Kleenex, her words muffled. "Can you all ever forgive me for being so selfish?"

Patrick walked around the bed to his sister's side and rubbed her shoulders as the fountain of tears continued. Bailey stood and reached across the bed to take her sister's hand. Victoria just rubbed her boney hand over her daughter's hair, while her own tears made streams down the side of her face. Her heart broke for her oldest child. She knew that the life she had led had affected Abigail the hardest. The question was not if she could forgive Abigail, but could Abigail forgive her?

Abigail's sobs finally subsided and she sat, still unable to control the shivers that shook her whole body. She prayed that she would never have to cry this much at once ever again. It was draining her. She felt as if she had run a marathon. Still dabbing at her eyes and taking deep breaths to try to get her shivers under control, she raised her head just a hair and locked eyes with her mother.

Victoria smiled at her oldest child. She thought back

at how Abigail had always seemed so grown up. Now here she was, looking so much like a child. "Sweetheart, you have nothing to feel guilty for. You were a child, thrust into an adult role. I can't tell you how proud I am of you, yet how sad I am that you had to lose so much of your childhood. I know that God's hand was on the situation the whole time, but that doesn't mean it was easy. It is I who would love to have your forgiveness for what I put you through."

"Oh, mother!" Abigail stood up and leaned over her mother's frail body to hug her. She held her body just inches over her mother and gently squeezed her shoulders. She wiped away the tears with the same Kleenex she had used to dab at hers and kissed her mother on the cheek. She placed her face right above her mother's and locked eyes once again. "Mother, I forgive you, if you'll forgive me."

Victoria wished so much that she had the strength left tonight to reach out and hug her daughter, but she didn't. She would just have to do the best she could to hug her with her eyes. "Of course, I will."

Bailey threw up her hands and exclaimed, "Great, Abigail, you've taken the spotlight away from me tonight! You'll owe me for this."

Abigail's head jerked back to look at her sister just in time to see that look of surprise as Patrick hurled the box of Kleenex at her. They all laughed and Victoria smiled as she closed her eyes and listened to the sound of their laughter.

"You look tired, mom," Patrick said as he caught the Kleenex box that Bailey was tossing back to him.

"I am. Would you mind if we continued our visit in the morning?"

"Of course not," Bailey said. "We want you to conserve all the strength you can through the weekend."

They each took turns giving their mother a kiss on the cheek and saying their goodnights. Victoria could hear them all talking at once and laughing as they climbed the stairs to their rooms. It was a sound she would never forget.

## Chapter 19

Abigail and Bailey were like new found friends. There was a girlish sound to their laughter as they laid across the twin bed that had been Bailey's childhood bed, shoulder to shoulder, catching up on what was currently going on in their lives.

Patrick had gone on past their door and to the next one in the narrow hallway. This was his old bedroom. He went in and sat on the side of his bed. He shook his head and grinned as he heard his sister's laughter through the wall. He was glad to see the tense look that was always on Abigail's face slowly start to turn into a look that said she was finding peace.

Peace. How do you find peace in the middle of this storm? His world had been turned upside down when he had learned of the cancer fourteen months ago. He thought it surely must be some cruel joke that was being played on him. He had never even seen his dad a day in his life and now his mother was going to leave him, too?

"God," Patrick whispered, "I would really love to find out that You are real. I sure could use a dose of whatever it is that You have given to the women of this house to make them seem as if they are okay with this situation. I feel so lost and out of place right now. I don't want to give my mother up just yet. I need her. But if she has to go, and there really is a chance that I could see her again someday, I want to figure out how I can make sure I'm there with her when my time is up."

He leaned back on his pillow trying to decide if he should go to bed, or crash the girl's room. His mother's Bible that he had left on the coffee table came to mind. He quietly went back down stairs to retrieve it.

Sarah was coming out of the den and almost ran Patrick over as he was coming out of the living room. "Oh, Patrick, you scared me!" Her high pitched voice said that she hadn't expected anyone else to be downstairs.

"I'm sorry, Sarah. I just forgot something."

Sarah looked at the Bible in his hand. She wanted to open her mouth and start talking to him, but something stopped her. She guessed what he needed right now was to find his own way. She thought he might be pretty close to making a decision, but maybe this was a time that needed to be just between him and God.

"That Bible is the one your mother uses the most. She has others, but that's the one she uses to study. I love reading the notes in the margins." A look of fond remembrance flashed across her eyes.

"I noticed those," Patrick said, his eyes focused on the Bible. "I'm not sure I understand what they mean, but I like reading them. You can almost feel the excitement she had when she wrote some of them." He looked Sarah in the eyes with the same lost little boy look he had earlier. "I'm trying to understand them. Really, I am."

Sarah gave him a compassionate smile and placed her hand on his arm. "God promises to give us wisdom when we ask for it. That means for you, too." She gave his arm a squeeze and went on down the hall to the kitchen. She would clean up and then go to bed. Victoria would be needing her in a few hours.

Patrick watched her walk down the hall. He felt like such an outsider. He looked back down at the Bible. Could this book really hold the answers he was seeking? He wasn't sure, but if they were in there, he'd find them. He made his way back to his room and decided he would get comfortable in the overstuffed chair his mother had put in his room when they first moved here.

That seemed like such a lifetime ago. He had been ten when they came to Texas. He was so used to them packing up and moving so often that it took him a couple of years to really consider this home. He tried not to get too attached to people or places. All of his life he was used to his mother coming home at least once a year and announcing that they were moving. She would be all excited and would promise they were finally going to be able to settle somewhere. That sounded nice, but settle somewhere for how long?

He had never really had any close friends. He hadn't been able to trust people very much. All he knew of people was that they leave. His father had left even before he was born. His dad had been his mother's last husband, but there had been plenty of boyfriends come in and out of their lives through the years. He was glad to see most of them go, but every once in a while there was one that he had allowed himself to start to trust. He had wanted a father to coach his soccer team and baseball team, someone he could talk to about guy stuff. He remembered

## No Regrets

when he needed his first jock strap. That was not the right thing to ask your mother and two older sisters to get for you. He was embarrassed to go in Wal-Mart for several months after they had made such a big scene. You would've thought they were shopping for a new car or something with all the questions they asked that poor man in the sporting goods department. But regardless of whether he liked one of his mother's boyfriends or not, the truth was still simply this, they would eventually be gone.

He remembered his mother telling him how Jesus wanted to be his friend. She told him that Jesus would never leave him, no matter what. He just hadn't ever been able to grasp the concept of how you could be close friends with someone that you couldn't see.

He finally got ready for bed and burrowed deep down within the chair. He opened up the Bible to where he had left off in Luke and continued to read. He read the entire book and still had so many questions, so many doubts. He knew he couldn't go to sleep if he laid down right now, so he started at the beginning of Luke again. After he had read through it three times he finally laid down for the night. As he drifted off he thought he heard the muffled sound of giggles. "Oh, surely they aren't still up," he mumbled to himself as his eyes closed. Their laughter was but a memory that would be recalled with a smile tomorrow.

## Chapter 20

Abigail looked over at her sister. She was sorry that she had missed so many years of these late night talks. She had thought of her siblings more as a chore she was responsible for instead of friendships to be cherished.

Bailey felt her sister's stare. "Do I have something hanging from my nose or what?"

Abigail fell on her side laughing. "Is everything a joke to you?"

"Sometimes. It's how I got through, you know."

"I know. Maybe it's a good thing. I wish I had laughed more."

The silence lingered between them for a few minutes. It was a comfortable silence that came with intimacy and understanding of each other.

Bailey looked at her sister with a seriousness in her eyes. "Do you think this condition that mother has will be passed down to one of us?"

"You mean you haven't already realized you've lost some of your mind?" Abigail looked out of the corner of her eye at her sister.

## No Regrets

"Oh! I can't believe you even said that!" She grabbed the pillow and in one fell swoop hit her sister across the head, laughing at the shocked look on Abigail's face as the pillow bounced off the side of her face.

Abigail's serious look came back on her face. "You're going to pay for that."

Bailey was afraid she had gone too far with her sister as Abigail got up from where they were laying. A look of regret washed across her face from having ruined this special moment between them. She was thinking how Abigail had never known the art of having fun and she had just pushed her back into her serious mode.

"Take that!" Abigail shouted as she pummeled the back of Bailey's head with the pillow from the other bed. The fight was on. These sisters who were now grown were finally learning how to play together.

The laughter finally subsided a short while later. Both girls were spent as they lay on their own beds, breathing heavy from the pillow fight.

"I don't want to be the kill joy, but we better get some rest so we can be there for mother tomorrow." Abigail was enjoying releasing the child in her, but she still knew her responsibilities.

"You're right. Besides, I don't want to hurt you too badly considering how much older you are than me."

Abigail turned her head to face her sister. "I may be older, but someday soon you'll see just how tough this *old* gal can be." With that she stuck out her tongue at Bailey, who was dramatically acting like she was scared by her sister's words.

They changed and crawled into bed and turned out the lights, but the whispering continued for quite some time.

## Chapter 21

Bailey was laughing at Abigail as she came into the kitchen and sat down at the bar. Her sister had a look similar to a hangover. You could definitely tell that she lived a life of someone much older than her thirty years. She smiled as she thought back to last night and the new friendship that had developed with her sister.

"Well, did you two finally go to sleep last night?" Patrick said, flipping some pancakes into the plate sitting in front of Bailey.

The two sisters looked at each with a look of conspiracy. "Yes," Abigail said, "But not until I *whooped* your sister good with my pillow."

Patrick just smiled. So that was why he felt the wall shake every once in a while. He was glad to see his sister's getting along so well. It's not that they had ever fought a lot, they were just at different ends of the spectrum when it came to their personalities.

Patrick had always been the best cook in the family. Abigail had done her best when she had to take care of them, but she hadn't been much of a cook. She had a tendency to even burn corn dogs. He loved the opportunities he had to cook for them these past months when they had all come home on the weekends.

"I just love your banana pancakes, Patrick. You really need to cook for me more when we're back in the city." Bailey said as she stuffed a huge bite into her mouth.

Patrick flashed her one of his heart stopping smiles. "Sure, sis. I'll cook for you once a week. I'm sure we could work out some type of exchange. Maybe laundry?"

"We'll see," said Bailey. "Laundry doesn't excite me, but it may be worth one of your meals."

Sarah walked into the kitchen, greeting each of the siblings that almost seemed like her own. She had smelled the aroma of Patrick's pancakes all the way in the den while she was tending to Victoria's morning routine. She had gently moved her to a chair while she changed the sheets, fluffed the pillows and made Victoria's bed as comfortable as possible. She would freshen up Victoria as well and comb her hair and put on one of the lovely silk bed jackets Abigail had bought for her when she first got sick. Victoria knew her body had wasted away, but it made her feel better to at least try to make herself presentable.

"What a wonderful smell, Patrick." Sarah said, breathing deeply, taking in the aroma of the pancakes.

"I'm glad you think so. I just finished making you a stack."

"You're a doll. I didn't get a chance to eat this morning before going in to see after your mother."

"How is she this morning?" Abigail asked, her eyes squinting in concern.

"She's in good spirits. I think she feels a weight has

been lifted off of her shoulders now that you know what she considered some dark shameful secret."

Bailey spoke up, still shoveling in her pancakes as if she hadn't eaten in days, "I'm not sure I understand what she was so ashamed of. She has a disorder. That wasn't her fault."

"True," Sarah said, pausing to finish chewing. She sat down her fork and looked up at them. "To us it's something that shouldn't be shameful, but to your mother there were so many different factors that rolled into one big ball of guilt and shame."

"What does she feel so guilty about? It wasn't easy on us to move around so much, deal with the men that came and went, or her erratic moods, but had we known a little bit more about why things were happening like they were, we could've been more understanding and supportive." Patrick had almost a look of hurt on his face.

"You have to remember that she didn't know why she was like she was, herself, until not too many years ago. Your mother was ashamed of her behavior the whole time she was raising you. She didn't know what drove her to do the things she did and she didn't know how to control it. She spent most of her life convinced that she was somewhat crazy. The burden of shame grew over the years. When she finally got the help she needed she was relieved, but still had the guilt of years she could not change. She also had to deal with allowing the memories of her own childhood to emerge. She had to deal with the knowledge and pain of the molestation. She also shared with me that she had a very hard time dealing with the fact that she had suffered all these years, as well as you three, because she took the burden and responsibility of what was done to her when it should not have been hers to bear. She resented that she felt like she had to carry that shame in order to protect the adults. She realized that in some ways she had passed that burden on to you. You had to take care of her so many times when she should've been taking care of you. That guilt and shame has eaten away at her almost as much as the disorder did through the years."

Abigail twirled her fork on her plate. "What can we do to convey to her that we love her more than any of all of this, that as far as our part in this we release her of any guilt? I know I have probably added to her guilt through the years by my remarks and actions, but I don't want her spending the little time she has left worrying about the past."

"Simply tell her. I think that's what she needs most right now. She knows in her heart that God has forgiven her for her past and she has forgiven those that have hurt her. She used all of her experiences in ways that have glorified God. She chose to let her pain enable her to ease other's pain. She's just holding on to the pain that she felt she caused you."

"Okay," Bailey said, standing up, "Let's get these horrible looks off of our faces and replace them with smiles and go give her a wonderful day." She grinned the biggest, fake grin she possibly could, breaking the somberness of the moment.

"You three go ahead, I'll clean up in here and join you in a bit." Sarah watched them walk away. She hadn't told them that she didn't think Victoria had much time left. Maybe she would tell them tonight. Let them enjoy today with their mother. While she gathered up dishes and begin washing pots and pans she turned her heart and voice to God. "God, I've wanted and prayed for things to happen the whole time You've had me here. I've tried to be patient and wait on Your timing, but it hasn't been easy. Once again, You're right on time. This is probably the last weekend that they will get to spend with their mother. All of the healing and restoration is finally happening after all. Abigail is learning to smile and laugh, even though she is in a very painful time of her life. Bailey is learning to have compassion for her sister. Maybe she'll be able to share more of her emotions with her sister now, instead of hiding them behind a smile. And Patrick. He's searching for You, God. He'll find You soon. I can feel it."

She finished up the kitchen and chose to spend a couple of minutes in the sun room with her Bible before going back to the den.

## Chapter 22

Victoria was slightly propped up on her pillows when they went in to see her. She barely had the strength to smile at her children, but she made the best effort she could. She wanted this day to be special.

They all gave their mother a kiss on the cheek, each taking turns telling her how pretty she looked or how she looked better today, anything to keep that smile that was barely noticeable.

Abigail pulled back the heavy drapes and pulled the blinds all the way up so that the sunshine flooded the room. Victoria noticed something very different about Abigail this morning. She seemed happy, truly happy. That dark countenance that usually shadowed her face was gone. She was such a lovely woman. Victoria had always thought that Abigail would've have been as pretty as any model if she would just take her hair down out of that pony tail she threw it up in every day. The girl had striking features, but she refused to wear any sort of makeup and kept such a serious look on her face. But today was different. Victoria took a second look at her. Her eyes could barely believe it, Abigail's hair was down and brushed forward, framing her face. She thought she even noticed a touch of mascara on her eyes.

As if reading her thoughts, Bailey came bounding over and whispered in her ear, "Do you like my creation?"

"She's beautiful," Victoria whispered, still staring at her oldest daughter as she was busy straightening up a few things and bringing chairs over near the bed for them to sit in.

"I thought so, too." Bailey had a look of love and admiration on her face as she watched her sister.

'God,' Victoria thought to herself, 'Have I already died and gone to heaven?'

All three children stood around her bed before sitting down. They had talked with each other before coming in and knew what they needed to do.

"Mother," Abigail said, as their spokesperson, "We forgive you." Victoria had a confused look on her face. "Mother," Abigail repeated, "We forgive you." Victoria looked at the other two standing around her bed. They were smiling and nodding their head in agreement. Victoria still had a confused look on her face and for a moment Abigail wondered if she hadn't understood her.

The tears that started to slide down the side of Victoria's face told them that she understood. They came in a steady stream now and all Victoria could do was look at each of her children, so thankful for this pardon, of sorts, they had just given her. That was the only part of her life that she felt was being left undone, and now it was done.

"Mother," Patrick said, "There's one more thing we need to hear from you before our time together is gone."

"Anything, darling. Anything for my precious babies."

"Good," Patrick continued, "Then you will forgive us?"

"Forgive you? For what?"

"For not being there for you and for each other the way we should have. For not seeing the pain of your life and not helping you carry that burden."

"Oh, baby, there's nothing to forgive you for."

"Yes, mother, there is," Abigail said as she lowered her face closer to her mother's. "We let you carry this pain around for all these years, regretting what you had done. We don't want you to have any regrets. We don't want any for ourselves, either. We don't want to have to carry around the knowledge that maybe there was something else we should've done to help you through life. No regrets, mother."

"I don't want you to go through that. It's a hard road to travel. So, yes, I forgive you. No regrets."

The tears were still coming down her face and Bailey was dabbing at them with a tissue as fast and as gently as she could. They all were crying now, even Patrick. Things had been settled between them all.

That day was the best day together that any of them could ever remember. They spent hours remembering the good times of their lives together. They pulled out all the old photo albums, even teased Victoria a bit about how there would be three hundred photos of one week and then no photos for a year. They played games and bantered back and forth, accused Patrick of cheating at cards, and laughed heartily at Bailey's jokes, even when they didn't get them. This was the family they had all long for.

## Chapter 23

They decided to have a cook out that night. They even put down several layers of blankets on the reclining lawn chair so that Victoria could join them. Sarah helped them rig up a makeshift IV pole. They weren't sure if Sarah would let them go through with idea, but she actually thought it would be good for Victoria.

Patrick carried his mother's almost weightless body outside and made sure she had plenty of covers. Victoria's smile seemed even wider tonight. She was completely loosed of the burdens she had carried around all these years. She should have taken care of it years ago.

Abigail was bringing the meat out to be cooked while Patrick was getting the grill ready. Bailey had brought out a radio and had music blaring. She grabbed Sarah and made her do some sort of chicken looking dance with her. Victoria couldn't ever remember Sarah being so silly. It was nice. It couldn't be easy on her to always be taking care of people that she knew would eventually die.

Patrick couldn't resist and dropped his spatula and joined the dance. Abigail continued back and forth between the kitchen, but this time when she came out Sarah grabbed the plate she was carrying and the other two grabbed their sister to come dance with them.

Abigail protested and tried her hardest to get out of this silliness, but her eyes caught a glimpse of her mother sitting over on the side watching. She remembered what Victoria had said to her in the letter. What was the song? I Hope You Dance. With tears in her eyes she succumbed to their pleas and joined them. She totally shocked them by twirling around to the music and completely letting herself go with the moment. Victoria thought about the song, too. "Dance, my little one," she whispered as a tear ran down her cheek.

They continued their party out on the back deck until after the sun had gone down. Sarah helped Patrick get his mother back to the den. Sarah was going to stay with Victoria, but she wouldn't hear of it. "Go enjoy yourself. Take a break. I'm going to sleep for a while and rest."

Sarah made sure that Victoria had her medications and was comfortable and then went back to join the other three.

They stayed out there late into the night watching fire flies and talking. Abigail, Bailey, and Patrick all sat lost in their thoughts for a bit, each thinking the same thing. Country life, there's nothing like it.

## Chapter 24

The next morning Bailey and Abigail came down dressed and ready for church. To their surprise Patrick sat at the bar drinking a cup of coffee, also ready to go to church. The sisters looked at each other wide eyed. They were used to Patrick making excuses to stay at the house while they went to church.

"Well, well, well, don't you look nice," Bailey said as she walked over to her brother and straightened his tie.

"Is this okay?" Patrick said, looking like he worried he had made a mistake. "I hadn't really brought any church clothes with me, but, believe it or not, mom still has some men's clothes tucked away in the attic. I found them last night and Sarah was nice enough to wash them before she went to bed and ironed them for me this morning. They're not the best fit, but I hope they'll do."

The sisters were still a little shocked, but thrilled. Who cared that the pants were a little too long and the shirt was a little big on him. He had rolled up the sleeves so that no one would know that the sleeves went all the way down to his fingers. "Are my cowboy boots okay to wear with this?" He said, looking down and assessing his look again.

"They're fine. You look perfect, Patrick." Abigail said, finally being able to move from her spot. She also noticed that he carried the Bible she had bought him last Christmas. 'Will miracles never cease?' She thought to herself, thanking God that her brother was even showing an interest.

He noticed them staring at him and started feeling red come to his cheeks. "If you two are going to stare at me the whole time, I'm not going."

"My, my, sir," Bailey said in her best southern belle voice, "We're just noticing a handsome gentleman standing in front of us. That's all. We'll avert our eyes as soon as the shock wears off."

He rolled his eyes and grabbed his Bible off of the counter. "Come on, you two. Don't you dare embarrass me today. You know this is all new to me."

"I promise I'll make your sister behave, Patrick. I may have to thump her on the back of the head like mother used to do us when we misbehaved in church, but I'll take care of her." Abigail gave her sister a look that said she meant it. This was probably the first time Patrick had been to church since he was made to go.

"You two are no fun. I promise to behave." The flash of love that flickered in her eyes when she looked at Patrick assured him that he was safe, at least at church. They said a quick goodbye to Victoria. The church was only a mile or so away, but they didn't want to be late.

The small church that their mother had attended since she moved here was nothing like the churches Abigail and Bailey were used to in the city. They loved the advantages of a large church, but there was nothing like coming home to this small group of people who had been worshiping together for decades. It felt comfortable. It felt like coming home.

Patrick was nervous. He wasn't sure why. He knew all of the people, had known them most of his life. Criar was the only town they had stayed in for more then a year. He tried to think back to how old he was when they had moved here. Ten? Eleven? He couldn't quite remember. He felt in awe now as he looked at the wood beams across the ceiling. It sure looked a lot smaller now. People were coming up to them and smiling and shaking hands and patting him on the back. He had the urge to bolt and run for a minute, but the genuineness of these people made him stay put.

# Chapter 25

Abigail was enjoying being at their old church again, but she could barely focus for wondering what Patrick was thinking. Was he listening closely? Was he keeping up with and understanding what the Pastor was saying? So many thoughts were going through her head that she couldn't even keep up with finding the scripture references. She was almost to the point of being flustered. She wanted to show him that it was good to take notes, that it's good if you turn to the scriptures along with the preacher so that you could learn the scriptures more for yourself. She wasn't being a very good example right now. Good thing he couldn't read her mind. He'd know that she had barely listened to a word that was said.

Patrick was completely entranced by what Pastor Tim was saying. The sermon was on Luke 12:1-12 today. He had read that the night before, but had some questions about things he wasn't sure he understood. Jesus had been talking about how nothing we did in secret would be hidden, how every little thing we did or said behind closed doors would be known. That had kind of spooked Patrick. He wasn't sure if he wanted God knowing everything he said or did. God would certainly be disappointed in him if He did, and would never want him on His side. He also had some concerns with verse nine where Jesus said that if we denied Him before men, He would deny us before God. Had he already blown that? There were so many questions that he needed to ask.

Bailey was a note taker. She had notes in the margins of her Bible, on bulletins, note pads, everywhere. They were organized chaos. No one else could've made sense of them, but she could. She wondered about her brother beside her. She would've sat back and tried to help him find the scriptures as they were read, but if she didn't write things down, she didn't comprehend them. She would just have to try to answer his questions later.

The sermon was coming to an end and both sisters were praying like they had never prayed before for their brother. Both of them had accepted Christ into their hearts in their teens, but Patrick just seemed to keep fighting it. At least his coming with them today was progress.

The invitation music began and Abigail reached for Bailey's hand. Bailey was so touched at her sister reaching out for her that she almost forgot to keep praying for Patrick. She opened her eyes while her head was still bowed. Patrick had a grip on the back of the pew in front of them like he was holding on for dear life. She was tempted to reach over and pry his fingers off the pew and give him a push, but she knew it was not her job. That was the job of the Holy Spirit. She would just continue to send up prayers for him from her heart.

The invitation had come to a close and Patrick was still in his seat. Both sisters found themselves a little dis-

## No Regrets

appointed, but kept reminding themselves that God's timing is perfect. When the music stopped and the closing prayer was said, people began to flock towards them. They were smothered in hugs from old Sunday School teachers and such. Patrick put his hand on Bailey's arm and mouthed, "I'll be right back." She acknowledged that she had understood him and then watched as he walked towards the back of the church where Pastor Tim was standing. The two of them shook hands and Pastor Tim stood there nodding as Patrick was talking and shuffling from foot to foot. When Patrick finished talking, Pastor Tim put his hand on his back and led him back toward the offices.

The hugs and handshakes seemed to go on forever. For a small church there sure were a lot of people to hug. Finally, the people started making their way out to their cars. Most of them would be heading to the local diners in town. Abigail and Bailey went back to the side parking lot where they had left their car and chose to just stand and lean against it rather than sitting inside where it was hot. They could barely talk. They didn't know whether to get excited or not. They were a little afraid, too. They knew Patrick was close to coming to a major decision in his life and they wanted it for him desperately, but they had to be patient and let God work.

About ten minutes later they saw Patrick come around the corner towards the car. They weren't sure what to make of his demeanor. His walk was confident, but he still had a very serious look on his face. He smiled at them and jumped in the car. "Come on girls, I'm hungry."

Abigail and Bailey just looked at each other. They would ask questions later.

# Chapter 26

There was almost a shadow over lunch that day. They would all be leaving and heading back to their separate lives. None of them wanted this weekend to come to an end. It had been almost magical. They weren't sure if they had ever been together where Abigail wasn't tense and Bailey wasn't almost fake with her laughter and Patrick wasn't fidgeting the whole time, wanting to get back to his buddies and his bars, but this time was different. They had experienced a soothing balm on their souls this weekend.

They took their time cleaning up the kitchen, making small talk as they went. Sarah came in and told Patrick that his mother would like to talk to him alone for a minute. The three girls just glanced at one another as he walked away.

When they heard the den door shut all three started talking all at once. When they realized that no one could make sense of all the clatter that was going on, they started laughing. They each got a cup of coffee and sat down at the table.

"I've been praying for your brother," Sarah said.

"Thank you," Bailey said. "You know we were late getting home because he went and talked to Pastor Tim for a while."

"Oh, really?"

"Yes, but he never said a word about what. We figured we should let him tell us when he's ready."

Abigail stared down at her coffee cup. "It's so hard just standing back and watching him struggle with this. I think what is hardest for me to accept is that I would love for him to come to Christ before mother is gone."

Sarah patted her hand. "Don't give up just yet."

There was a quiet pause as each woman got lost in her own thoughts, sipping their coffee. Sarah looked up at the other two. "I don't think your mother will last much longer." They didn't say anything. The look on their faces said that they knew she was right.

Abigail ran her finger around the rim of her coffee cup. "Is there anything else we can do to make it easier for her?"

"I think you've given her what she needed this weekend. When she goes it will be with a peaceful heart now. You can take comfort in that."

"I'm not sure I can let her go just yet. I still need her." Bailey's eyes were filling with tears.

Her sister reached for her hand a second time today. "We don't have a choice, Bailey. I don't want to give her back to God either, but it's not our choice. I do promise you this, though, I will always be there for you. We'll be there for each other."

"I thought you didn't like having to take care of us," Bailey teased.

"I thought a lot about that last night. Maybe God allowed me to go through that so I would know how to take care of you now. He was shaping me and preparing me."

"What do you think God was preparing me for?"

Abigail thought for a moment and then looked up at her sister with a smile. "I think God has prepared you to remind us to laugh. I need that."

"I might can handle that," she grinned back.

Sarah didn't want to interrupt this moment, but she couldn't help it, her heart was welling up with emotion, too. "I'm going to miss this family so much."

Both girls reached out for Sarah's hands. "You've been an angel to this family, Sarah." Bailey nodded her agreement with her sister's statement.

Tears filled Sarah's eyes. This was always the hard part, letting go. "Your mother has stolen my heart with her love and compassion for people. She may not have let go of her own pain, but she never let it stop her service to God. For the first few months that I was here she had her weekly Bible study come out here. She kept her position on the board for the women's shelter as long as she could hold out. When she couldn't go to church she would write cards of encouragement to those God laid on her heart. She's been such a blessing to me. I've also had the chance to pray with her many times. Your three names were on her lips constantly. She constantly pleaded for God to take care of you. You're very fortunate to have her. My mother died when I was very young."

"I'm so sorry, Sarah, I didn't know that." Abigail realized that they had never really asked Sarah much about herself.

They heard the den door open and Patrick's footsteps coming down the hall.

## Chapter 27

When Patrick walked into his mother's room she was looking towards the window, deep in thought. He felt like he did in school when he was called to Principal's office when he hadn't known he had done anything wrong. He leaned over and gave her a kiss on the cheek.

"Pull up a chair, Patrick, let's have a talk."

He did as he was told, moving the chair up towards the head of the bed. He didn't want her to have to strain herself talking anymore than she needed to. He took her hand and waited.

"Patrick, I want to ask you if you've come to know Christ yet."

She sure didn't waste any time getting to the point, did she? He thought a minute, trying to figure out how to answer that. "Not yet, but I talked to Pastor Tim today and he answered a lot of questions that I had."

"Do you have any other questions that maybe I could help you with?"

"One thing that I'm afraid of is having to change my life so much, pretty much completely."

"Why is that, Patrick? What part do you think would be too hard to give up?"

"I don't know. I know my life is pretty empty right now. There's not much worth keeping. My friends are only around when the beer is flowing. I have a two bit job that anyone off the street would be qualified for. I had a dream once, but it quickly faded."

"What was your dream?"

"I always wanted to help people, maybe be a Paramedic."

"A Paramedic?" There was a bit of a surprise in his mother's voice.

"Yes. Silly, huh?"

"Not at all, son. That's a very commendable profession. What stopped you?"

"I was afraid."

"Afraid of what?"

"Afraid of failing."

"I know that feeling. I learned something very important over the span of my life. You only truly fail when you don't try."

"I guess so, but it's too late now."

"Too late? You're only twenty-three, Patrick. You have your whole life ahead of you. It's never too late to follow your dreams. I didn't even really begin to go after mine until I was in my forties."

"That's true. I just don't know if I have the strength to carry it through."

"Patrick, I want to tell you something that I needed to hear over and over for many years, that I wished I had told you and your sisters over and over throughout the years. I believe in you. I believe that you can and will make the right choices. I believe that you can be a

Paramedic and be the best around. I believe in you, son. Never forget that."

The tears were starting to form in his eyes now. He didn't want to cry today. When he left he wanted everyone to have smiles on their faces. No more tears for now.

"Now, Patrick, are there any other questions or concerns about God?"

"Yes, one. You've always told me that God is a Father to the fatherless. I'm not sure I understand that."

"There are so many aspects to God. He is the Healer, Protector, Comforter, and so much more. He is everything that we need Him to be. He is also a parent to us. He is God the Father. When we accept Him into our hearts, He adopts us. We are His children. We'll never stop being His child, just like you'll never stop being my child. Not all fathers on earth know how to make us feel safe and secure and loved, but God is the perfect Father. He loves us when we need love. He disciplines us out of that love when we need it. We can crawl into His lap and feel His arms around us and know that He's there. I want that for you, Patrick. I know you've always longed for a father. He is your answer."

"How can I crawl into the lap of someone I can't see or feel?"

"You'll know when you finally let yourself go to Him. It's a feeling of warmth and love like you've never experienced."

Patrick wondered if that could really be true. He wished more than anything that it could be.

"You're my baby boy, Patrick. I love you so much. Please don't wait too long to make this decision."

"I'm working on it, mother."

"Do me one last favor, son."

"Anything for you."

"Take care of your sisters. They may be older than you, but they will need a strong shoulder to cry on and a strong arm to hold them up in this life. Be there for them and let them be there for you."

"I will, mother. I love those two, even if I don't always show it. I'll work on showing it more."

"Why don't you go get your sisters. I'd like to spend a little more time with all of you before you have to go."

"Sure" He rubbed his thumb across the back of her hand. He wanted to remember every little thing about her. He didn't want to forget the way she smelled like lilacs or the sky blue color of her eyes. He really didn't want to let go of her hand, but he didn't want to be selfish with this time. He finally released her hand and went to find his sisters.

## Chapter 28

Sarah let them go in by themselves while she went to sit in her favorite spot, the sun room. She had almost become so attached to this family that she felt a little left out. Another week or so and she wouldn't just be done with her job, she'd be left behind by four people who had become very dear to her. She'd move on to yet another family, and eventually be left again.

She knew she was just feeling sorry for herself. This wasn't about her, this was about them, about making their lives as comfortable and easy as possible through what is already a difficult situation.

Sarah was only seven when she lost her mother in a car accident. They had taken her and pretty much dropped her on her father's doorstep, but he had a job that put him on the road most of the time, and his new wife didn't much care for taking care of this child she had never really been around. Sarah had only seen her father three times in the five years her parents had been divorced. So it wasn't long until her grandmother had picked her up and taken her back to live with her. Her grandmother lived alone in a very small apartment in a part of the city that wasn't exactly suitable for a seven year old girl, but there wasn't much that could be done about that.

Sarah worked hard in school. She put herself through college by babysitting at night during the weeks, which was great because she usually got to do her homework and studying. Then she worked as a waitress on the weekends. She had wanted to be a nurse for as long as she could remember. She loved people and never wanted anyone to feel alone, the way she had, while they were coming to the end of their life.

Her grandmother had died three years ago. Sarah had never felt more alone. It was then that she had turned to God. She was desperate to have someone in her life again. She felt totally abandoned. God had come to her one night in her apartment while she cried, pouring out her heart.

She had people that would come into her life and she would come to love, but they would always leave. This family was different. Victoria was the godliest woman she had ever known and had taught her so much about God the past fourteen months. She had taught her all about prayer and Sarah had never felt closer to anyone ever before in her life.

Victoria's daughters had been the sisters she had never had. She loved them dearly and couldn't wait until they were due for another visit.

Patrick was another story altogether. He had a smile that almost made her dizzy, but she would never let him know that. He had asked her out a couple of times, but she had declined. She promised God that she would never get involved with anyone who wasn't a Christian. She had prayed for him the whole time she knew him, not

## No Regrets

just because of her attraction to him, but mainly because she cared about what happened to his soul.

Maybe she should just go to work at a hospital where the patients came in and out too often to get attached. She could get a dog to keep her nights from being so quiet. She had thought these thoughts a thousand times, but she knew it didn't matter what her plans entailed, she would go where God led.

# Chapter 29

All three children lingered in their mother's room. No one wanted to say goodbye. They knew they would be back in five days, but there was a bond between them that wasn't there before. They knew their time was coming to an end with their mother and they didn't want to waste precious time on their individual lives that seemed so insignificant right now.

Victoria was very weak today and in great pain, even with the pain medication. She was doing her best to not let how she felt show in her face. She had a feeling that this would be the last time she saw her children this side of heaven and she wanted smiles on their faces.

Bailey was smoothing her mother's hair with her hand. "Maybe next weekend Abigail and I can doll you all up, fix your hair and makeup. We'll have a makeup party." Bailey sure wished she could use her charm right now to make everyone laugh. Maybe laughter can't fix everything. Maybe she shouldn't try to fix everything. There's times that nothing you can say can make them funny. This was one of those times. "Mother, I'm scared."

"I know sweetheart. I want you to remember that it's okay to be scared. Just remember that God is still in control, no matter how scared you get. The storms of life may continue on around us, but God has you in His hand. The storm may get you wet, but it can't overtake you."

Bailey smiled down at her mother. "I'll remember that."

Abigail stood beside her sister, their arms touching. Victoria couldn't remember a time when they looked so happy being with each other. "Don't worry, Mother," Abigail said. "When the time comes I'll take good care of her."

"I know you will, Sweetheart." Victoria smiled at her oldest child. "But promise me that you will also let her take care of you. You both have something that the other needs."

The girls looked at each other and smiled. Their mother had never been so proud. Patrick walked over from where he was looking out the window.

"Is this an all girls club or are men allowed?" Patrick said putting his arms around his sister's shoulders.

"If you promise to cook for me this week I'll make sure you're given a special pass." Bailey looked over her shoulder at her brother.

Patrick just raised his eyebrows. "That might can be arranged. I hate to say it, but it's about time for me to get going."

"You'll remember our talk?" His mother said, her eyes pleading to him.

"Yes, Mother. I'll do my best to try to find the answers I need."

"God will give them to you. Just listen closely for

His voice."

Patrick nodded. He gave both of his sister's a kiss on the cheek and playfully tosseled their hair. He stepped around to the other side and leaned down to kiss his mother's cheek. "I love you," he said, still hovering close to her face.

"I love you, too, Patrick." Her voice was sounding so weak.

He walked to the door and turned to give them one last look. "I'll see you all next week. Bailey, call me this week and we'll see about getting you that dinner."

"Sure. You know I won't miss the opportunity for a home cooked meal." Bailey said.

Patrick walked out the door and was getting his bags that he had left at the bottom of the stairs. He saw Sarah sitting in the sun room, deep in thought. "Hey, Sarah. Are you okay in here? You look like you are far away."

Sarah was pulled from her thoughts. "I'm okay." She looked up and noticed just how handsome he was with the sun shining on him like a spot light. What in the world was up with these thoughts she was having of him today? "You have a safe trip, Patrick."

"Thanks, I will." He flashed her one last dazzling smile and turned to leave. His thoughts were still on Sarah as he got in his car. He knew she was something special, but how could he ever express that to her without sounding like he was at a bar trying to picking her up? She knew where he was at in his life, but did she realize things were changing for him?

The girls stayed with their mother another twenty minutes before saying their goodbyes. They found Sarah and gave her a hug. She was so much like another sister to them. They had talked last night about asking her to

# No Regrets

stay in touch with them when her job here was done. They would talk to her about it next weekend.

The house was so quiet with everyone gone. Sarah went back in and made sure Victoria was as comfortable as possible. The medicine was barely doing anything for the pain anymore, but it shouldn't be much longer. Sarah visited with her for a few minutes before leaving her to take a nap. Her strength was gone. She needed to rest as much as possible now.

Sarah went back to her spot in the sun room. She would need to strip the beds and get the house ready for their next visit, but right now she just needed to sit and talk to God.

## Chapter 30

When Patrick walked in the door of his apartment he was met with a pungent smell, probably from not taking out the trash before he left and stale cigarette smoke from the ash trays his friends frequently used. Somehow it was different walking in this time. The smell nauseated him and the site of beer cans scattered here and there looked more like they belonged in someone else's apartment. He was headed towards the kitchen to get a trash bag to begin cleaning up when he noticed his answering machine blinking. He had 17 calls. Didn't these people ever listen to him talk about how sick his mother was and him going to visit her? All the messages were pretty much the same, telling him they were having a party here or at this bar, come join them. He hit the erase button. What once had filled his weekends now repulsed him.

Once he finished cleaning up and opening the windows to let out the stale air, he sat down on his couch. He started thinking. If he was going to leave behind his old life, what would be his new life? He went over and over the conversation his mother and he had about his becoming a paramedic. Could he really go back to school? He would have to give up his job, not that it was worth hanging on to. Where would he take classes? He didn't really like the colleges around here, they intimidated him. He would rather go to a small junior college to start out. Now how in the world did he think he was going to quit his job, move off to a smaller town and support himself while he took classes? His dream was fading into the background fast.

What was that his mother had said, the only real failure is when we don't try? "Oh, mother," Patrick said to himself, "I don't want to give up. I'm just not sure how to move forward with this." A scripture his mother used to quote came to mind; *With men this is impossible, but with God all things are possible.* He thought he was finally starting to realize what that meant. For so many years he had looked to himself to lead the way, but that was getting him no where. Maybe it was time to stop holding out for a miracle of some sort and just give God the reigns. God couldn't possibly do any worse with his life than he had.

Right there, in his small, stale living room, Patrick got down on his knees and cried out to God. "God, I'm not sure how I'm suppose to do this. I've heard my mother speak of how to become a Christian many times, but I wasn't listening too well at the time. All I know is that I have made a mess of my life. I need You, God. I need You to lead me and guide me. I need You to show me how to live so that I can be happy. Pastor Tim told me that I could be a new creation, start over from here. That's what I want, God. I want You to be the friend to me that I hear my sisters, and my mother, and Sarah talk about. Most importantly, God," his chin began to quiver, "I need You to be the Father I never had. Save me, Jesus. Amen." He stayed in the floor for what seemed an eternity. He was afraid to move. There was this warmth and peace surrounding him and he was afraid it would disappear if he moved. He thought about how his mother had said he would know when God held him. This was the first hug from God that Patrick had been aware of in his life. He prayed that it wouldn't be his last.

He felt so excited! He felt like the weight of the world had been lifted off of his shoulders and like a veil had been lifted. His path for the future was becoming clearer, too. Tomorrow he would clean out his locker at work and get some information on a few colleges he wanted to check on down around where his mother lived. That country life had felt really good to him, somehow right. Maybe it was time to make some major changes. A sadness fell over him when he realized that he didn't have any friends that he could call and tell the big news of his new found life. He could call his mom, and she would be thrilled, but he thought maybe he would take care of some things here tomorrow and then surprise her Tuesday and tell her the news in person. She would be so proud.

That night he was being bombarded with so many calls from people wanting him to go to the bars. He couldn't believe how much that even the mere thought of that disgusted him. He finally shut off his phone around 10:00 and went to bed. He had a lot to do this week, and he was anxious to get started.

## Chapter 31

Bailey had thought long and hard about the weekend. She could not recall having such a good time with her brother and sister. She wished that Abigail lived a little closer so that they could hang out a little more, but she wasn't so far that they couldn't get together fairly regularly. She let her mind drift to thoughts of moving closer to Criar, further away from the city. There was still a magical spell cast on her from staring out into the vast, dark night with a million twinkling eyes staring back at her. The hustle and bustle of city life didn't seem near as glamorous as she fought the traffic coming back home. The sun was starting to set, but you could see no stars, just a pink haze hovering over the sky scrapers of downtown. Commuting wouldn't be so bad, would it? She would have to pray about that.

Her stomach was growling. She should've stopped somewhere on the way home. She knew without a doubt that she had nothing in her refrigerator that wouldn't double as penicillin. She hoped if she ever married, he would know how to cook. That really wasn't her forte. If it couldn't be served to her by a waiter, or picked up, or delivered, it was foreign to her. Chinese it was. She didn't feel like getting back out tonight, so she could have that delivered. She couldn't wait for Patrick to cook for her this week. Where had he learned to do that? I guess it didn't matter as long as he did, and she was close enough to enjoy it.

She had finished unpacking when the Chinese was delivered. After she filled her stomach she would take a long hot bath and relax. She didn't have to be at work tomorrow. She had turned in some designs to be looked over Friday before she left, just in case she had needed to stay.

She was finally full enough to take the leftovers to the refrigerator and put them away for tomorrow's lunch. She really needed to throw everything away that was unrecognizable tomorrow, which would be just about everything.

She let out a long groan as she sank down into the hot bath. She hadn't realized just how tight her muscles were until they were allowed to relax and let the water hold them up. She leaned her head back over the curve of the back of the antique claw-footed tub that she loved and put a gel eye pack over her eyes. Now, this is relaxing. She wondered if Abigail ever did anything for herself to help her relax and unwind. She would have to take some things with her next week and teach her the art of enjoying mud masks and bubble baths. She would paint her sister's toes a bright pink, betting that Abigail had never even considered the color. She would call her sister tomorrow and tell her to prepare for a weekend of spa treatments. She would call Sarah, too. She needed someone to pamper her as well. Bailey was surprised to find that she missed Sarah almost as much as she did Abigail.

## No Regrets

It was all settled. Next weekend would be times of pedicures and manicures and facial treatments. She would even wax their eyebrows. Now, that would be a surprising treat, or at least a surprise. She would go shopping tomorrow and get everything they would need. She thought she might even get them all a new big, fluffy terry cloth robe and slippers to complete the spa affect. They could do this in their mother's room so that she could enjoy the laughter that was sure to be flowing as well. They might could even paint her fingernails and toenails.

"I might not know how to cook like Patrick or handle my money and my life like Abigail," she said out loud to herself, "but I can pamper a person and make them feel fabulous!" she said, throwing up her arms and sending water flying. She giggled to herself. The new found friend she had discovered in her sister had made her feel excited about life for the first time in a long time. Not a fake excitement, covered by fake smiles, this was genuine.

## Chapter 32

Abigail walked into her apartment to find everything just as she had left it, perfect. She never let anything get out of place. Her cat, Princess, came bounding out of her bedroom, obviously excited to see her. The woman next door looked after Princess when Abigail was gone, but Princess was a one person cat by all means. Princess was a white Persian with the brightest, clearest green eyes you've ever seen. Her name fit her well. She pranced around like she was queen of this home. Abigail sat her luggage inside the door and took time to give Princess some attention. She had left her mother's the same time as Bailey, but she had a longer drive. She was so tired that she didn't even bother with getting any dinner. She just wanted to unpack and go to bed.

When she finally got things settled and sank down into her soft silk sheets, she couldn't help but to smile as she remembered the late night talks with Bailey that still lingered in her head. That girl could see humor in everything. She remembered how it felt to smile and giggle late into the night. She didn't want that feeling to fade.

## No Regrets

She wanted to have more of those times in her own life. She was thinking of the pillow fight, the first in her life, as she drifted off to sleep.

That morning she was rushing around trying to get dressed. The alarm clock had failed to go off. She was sure she had set it. She reached for one of her dark business suits and stopped. Bailey would think that was totally uptight. She reached, instead, for a flowing floral skirt and a soft pink sweater. She took a little extra time with her make-up, making it soft and feminine and then hunted for the old curling iron that she knew was somewhere and fixed her hair to frame her face the way that Bailey had taught her. She took one last look in the mirror, barely recognizing herself, and headed off to work.

She had a bounce to her step as she stepped off of the elevator onto the fifth floor, which was where her firm was. She went through the lobby area, smiling at the front receptionist, who could only reply with a surprised look. The back offices consisted of a long hallway with offices and conference rooms, all enclosed with glass walls. There were some offices that had their blinds drawn, but most were opened. Abigail waved or smiled at those she made eye contact with and more than one person got up and went to their window to see if that was actually their stiff necked, uptight Abigail.

Abigail came to another lobby area. There were four secretaries that took care of everything from coffee to setting up meetings for the different accountants. Her secretary's name was Lacey. Lacey had been very intimidated by Abigail at first, and still was at times, but she had learned what Abigail liked and disliked. That had helped a lot. Her first few weeks working for Abigail had been horrible. She had left the office almost every day in tears because she wasn't sure how to please her boss. As Abigail approached the desk to retrieve her messages, Lacey jumped, hitting her knee on the desk drawer that was pulled out.

"Hello, Miss Westbury, how was your weekend?" Lacey said nervously.

"Please, call me Abby, and my weekend was wonderful. Thank you. How was your weekend, Lacey?"

Lacey almost didn't know what to say. Abigail had never been anything but formal with her and had not made small talk with her before. "It was fine, thank you. Can I get you some coffee?" Lacey said, trying to make sure she didn't get too relaxed.

"No, thank you," Abigail replied, "I'll get some in a minute when I've had a chance to look through my mail." Abigail gave her a smile and went into her office, leaving Lacey bewildered, but pleased.

## Chapter 33

Patrick had gone to his work place and told them he was sorry, but that he was moving on, cleaned out his locker, and said goodbye to a few friends. He had tried to explain to them this new life that he was embarking on with God leading the way, but they just looked at him with a look in their eyes that told him they weren't even interested in hearing about it. "Maybe someday, God, you can use me to reach out to them." Patrick said to himself as he loaded the small box of things that had cluttered his work life. Most of the things he just threw in the trash. He had no desire for the calendars that exploited women on them or the hats and magnets that advertised what had been his alcohol of choice. He couldn't believe the transformation that had occurred just overnight. His desires for his life had totally changed. He was headed now to check out a few of the colleges around here and see what type of paramedic programs they had or what he even needed to do to pursue that career when he got the call.

"Patrick, it's Bailey." His heart froze, refusing to beat when he heard the quiet sniffles. "She's gone. Sarah just called me about ten minutes ago. She said she went peacefully in her sleep this morning."

Patrick was hearing the words, but not comprehending them. This couldn't be. He was going to surprise his mother tomorrow with the news of him giving his heart to God. She had wanted to know that before she died and he had the chance to tell her, but didn't. There was a burning pain deep within his gut.

"I'm going to call Abigail and then I'll be heading out for Criar. Would you like for us to ride together?" He had heard what she said, but couldn't answer. "Patrick, are you okay?"

He shook his head to clear it. "Yes, sis. I'm okay, just stunned. I know we've been preparing for this moment, but I still wasn't ready for it."

"I understand." Bailey whispered.

"I'll head out there on my own when I get home and get packed. Will you be okay to drive?" Patrick said.

"Yes," replied Bailey, "I think the drive will be good for me. It will give me time to think before I get there."

"Okay, sis, I'll meet you there. Please, be careful." Patrick said, already lost in his own thoughts.

"I will." said Bailey.

Patrick was numb. Why had he waited to tell his mother of his becoming a Christian. It would've made her so happy. Now he'd never get the opportunity. Regret and guilt made the blood run course through his veins. "See, God," he said looking up, "I can't even do this right. How in the world am I going to do what it takes to become a paramedic?"

He ran by the apartment, got what he needed, and hit the road. As he berated himself for not calling his mother last night it was if God gently tapped him on the

## No Regrets

shoulder and reminded him that he would see his mother again. That was a great comfort. He just regretted not letting her know that he had granted her last request. That would haunt him for the rest of his life.

When he drove up to the house he could see that Bailey had just gotten there a little bit ahead of him. She still had her bags on the porch and was hugging Sarah. His body became like jelly. He didn't think he could step out of his truck and walk up those steps knowing that his mother was no longer there.

Sarah stood on the porch after Bailey went in, waiting for Patrick to walk up, but he was just sitting in his truck, staring. She walked out to his truck and opened the driver's side door. "Are you alright, Patrick?" She said, worrying that he might pass out. He just shook his head and started to cry. He turned in his seat to embrace her and as he cried she just held him, whispering comforting words into his hair. She had never seen him show his emotions like this. The tears rolled down her own face as she continued to hold him.

After several minutes passed, his sobs finally quieting, he let go of the bear hug in which he had taken Sarah and looked so shy and embarrassed. Another thing she had never seen in association with Patrick. She handed him a Kleenex and let him regain his composure before she walked him up to the house. It wasn't much longer before Abigail arrived and the three siblings spent time embracing and crying over the loss of their mother.

# Chapter 34

That evening was very somber. The members of the church their mother had belonged to had brought enough food by the house to last them a month. People came and went, giving them hugs, taking their hands, telling them how very special their mother was. If it hadn't been so touching, it would've been annoying. Pastor Tim and his wife were the last to linger. They needed to talk to him about the funeral arrangements, but that could wait until morning.

When everyone was gone, all four of them were left sitting at the dining table, staring at the mounds of food. The silence hung in the air like the early morning fog on a cool day. Everyone was lost in their thoughts. Patrick started to sob again, a heart wrenching sob that was so out of character for Patrick. It took the girls by surprise to be sure. They all reached out and placed their hands on top of his, letting him release the flood of tears that could not be stopped. It seemed like hours before he was able to slow down his breathing and look up at the three women who were there at the table. He thought he must look pretty silly since it was suppose to be him being the strong one and comforting them. It was just his guilt of not picking up the phone and calling his mother that was weighing on his heart so heavily.

"I've made a horrible mistake," he blurted out as he wiped his eyes and blew his nose. This made all the girls sit up a little taller with curiosity. They couldn't imagine what he had done that was so bad just since he had left them yesterday. They waited patiently, even though they had a deep urge to start throwing questions at him. He sat there for a short while, his eyes red and puffy. Finally he spoke. "I gave my heart to God last night," he said in a matter of fact fashion.

The girls all jumped up and were hugging him. Words were flying so fast that you couldn't understand a word that was being said. When they finally settled down a tad their faces were plastered with huge smiles. They couldn't be prouder for him. So why was he still looking like he might break down and cry again?

"Patrick," Abigail said softly, "this is fantastic news. Why are you so upset about it?"

He sat there for a minute, chin quivering. When he finally spoke, it was as though he had been handed down a death sentence. "I didn't call Mother. She didn't get to know that before she died." The tears silently rolled down his face.

"But Patrick," Bailey said with a smile, "the Bible says that there is joy in the presence of the angels of God over one sinner who repents. Mother is with the angels. You can bet she is rejoicing most of all!"

Patrick stopped wiping his eyes and looked at her. "Where have I heard that before?" Patrick asked.

"It's in Luke," Sarah said, "the book of the Bible your mother had you reading."

A look of recognition came over Patrick's face as the realization of what he had just heard sunk in. His mother knew. He could now celebrate his new life with no regrets.

The next couple of days were a blur. There wasn't a lot to do in preparing for the future because Victoria had talk to Pastor Tim and had taken care of that ahead of time. Sarah was such a blessing during this time. She saw that the den was cleared of all medical objects and returned to its former appearance. She promised the girls that she would stay for a few days after the funeral and help them clear up a few things at the house. She wasn't quite sure how she was going to handle leaving this family. She had grown closer to this one than any other family she had ever worked for. She didn't think she could go back to work again for a while. She needed time to let her heart heal before she could let others in.

The funeral was a wonderful tribute to Victoria's life. The small church was packed to capacity and people were even standing outside. The children had no idea just how much Victoria's life had impacted this community. They made sure that Sarah sat with them. None of them would hear of her sitting in the back by herself among strangers. She was one of them now whether she knew it or not. She was sitting beside Patrick who had a protective arm around Bailey with his hand touching Abigail's shoulder. It was strange that there was such a major difference in Patrick in such a short amount of time. He had definitely been made into a new creation. When Pastor Tim started naming the family members and speaking to them about their mother, Patrick reached over and took Sarah's hand. She felt sure that he was just including her among them. Wasn't he?

## No Regrets

Victoria was being buried in the cemetery at the church, so they all walked somberly out there behind the pall bearers. There were so many flowers that the church had been overflowing and the grave site was also flooded with bouquets of flowers and plants. The grave side service would be simple and consist only of Pastor Tim reading a passage from Psalms and one of the church members that had a beautiful voice would sing *Amazing Grace*. She did a wonderful job with the song. Her voice was deep and rich. When the grave side service was over there was yet another outpouring of hugs and condolences. Bailey longed for the haven of the house so that she could just allow herself to feel the heartbreak she was feeling right now.

A man walked up to Patrick, looking a little unsure of himself. Patrick extended his hand like he had everyone else and just kind of nodded out of the habit of repetition. The man shook his hand in return, but just continued to stand there and look at him strangely.

"Is there something I can do for you?" Patrick asked with caution, not sure how to respond to the man's stare.

"No. I'm sorry for your loss." the man replied and walked away.

Patrick thought just how strange that was, yet the man seem to have a familiarness to him. Patrick stood watching him walk away. The thought of this stranger flooded Patrick's thoughts the rest of the day.

## Chapter 35

There would be a lot to do at the house. It was almost overwhelming. There were so many things that needed to be gone through and cleaned out. They had all agreed that their mother's clothes should be donated to the women's shelter. She would've liked that. They were still eating on leftovers from well wishers and probably could for the entire week, if they didn't get sick of them first. Patrick had gone back to his duty as cook for breakfast, for which they were all thankful.

They had taken up the habit of meeting in the den where their mother had been for fourteen months and had a devotional and prayer before they started anything. Patrick especially enjoyed this time because there was so much he wanted to know about. He couldn't take it in fast enough.

That first afternoon they had decided to start in the attic. No one had been up there in so many years. They weren't even sure what their mother had stored up there. As expected, it was very dusty and cobwebs were abundant. Everything seemed organized, as was their mother's way.

## No Regrets

There were boxes in one corner that were labeled with each sibling's name. In these they found childhood toys that they had thought were long gone, and baby clothes. She had saved outfits from birth up until they were old enough to start discarding and trading out clothes in their closets by themselves. They laughed about outfits that they couldn't believe they had owned, let alone worn. Had Abigail really owned a pair of orange bell bottoms? What about those tiny go-go boots of Bailey's! They all gave Patrick a hard time about the silk shirts with the wide collars that he had worn in about the fifth grade. Of course, there were a few tears shed over special outfits from their childhood. She had even saved the little dress that Bailey wore when she was five years old and carried the flowers for the homecoming queen.

Victoria had also divided up all of the pictures of each child and had put them in photo albums for them. When had she had time to do all of this? There were also photo albums full of pictures of their relatives that had died years ago. She had done a wonderful job of separating them out so that each child could have pictures of their grandparents and other deceased relatives. Each child's box also included pictures of their fathers.

Patrick stopped cold in his tracks. The only time he had seen a picture of his father was when he was young. He hadn't wanted anything to do with the man that had walked out on him before he was born. He stared at the photo. Where had he seen this man before? Maybe it was just a memory that had been tucked in the recesses of his mind all these years. The very thought of him brought up feelings that now felt foreign to his body. How was he supposed to deal with these feelings now that he was a Christian. He wasn't sure how he could forgive his father, even though he knew he would have to eventually.

They found trunks of things that had belonged to their grandparents. There was jewelry of their grandmother's that had been wrapped in velvet and tucked away in a jewelry box. Why hadn't their mother worn any of this? Their grandfather's Bible that he had used was wrapped in tissue. It was so well worn that the binding had been held together with tape. There were trinkets and just a hodgepodge of things their grandparents had collected over the years.

Sarah was enjoying going through the boxes with them. She didn't have anything left of her mother's and only kept her grandmother's Bible and her favorite figurine of a ballerina stretching up towards heaven, balanced on her toes. That was all the memories she had left of her family. Beyond that she was all alone in this world.

Bailey squealed in delight. "Look what I found! She held up matching outfits that her and her mother had used to dress up in at Halloween and sometimes just to put on a show for the rest of the family. They had both dressed up as Shirley Temple one time and fake tap danced their way through *The Good Ship Lollipop*. She had even kept the pink tutus they had made so they could twirl around the living room like they were ballerinas in a rendition of *Swan Lake*. Her mother had even made her Barbie's outfits to match sometimes. There were also the times when her mother would help her dress up in her clothes and high heels. She would put big floppy hats on her head and a feather boa around her neck and would give them all a fashion show. There was a pink feather boa in the box. Bailey took it out and wrapped it around her neck. She thought she could still

## No Regrets

smell her mother's perfume on the boa.

Abigail quietly went through her box. Her mother had kept all the books that she had immersed herself in. That was Abigail's way of coping. She would hide in her room or whatever quiet corner she could find and read for hours on end. She would pretend that she was characters in these books and she would take herself to faraway lands and live in houses full of beautiful things and with a big family that all loved each other and was there for each other. Sometimes she would be a Princess and the King would dote on her and lavish her with gifts as well as his love. Abigail's mother would try to get her to join her and Bailey in their fashion shows, but Abigail thought they were silly and almost resented them for playing around so much instead of doing some of the chores that she would have to do when her mother wasn't able. She wished terribly now that she had played more with them while she had the chance. She couldn't change the past, but she was going to make sure she changed the future.

"Hey," Sarah said, "does anyone know whose truck that is down there?"

Patrick jumped up and went to the window. It was an older truck with a man sitting in it, the same man from the funeral. "I'll take care of this." He said, headed towards the stairs.

## Chapter 36

Patrick wasn't sure what was going on, but he was about to find out. He took the stairs of the porch two at a time and walked out to the truck. The man stepped out, still looking unsure of himself.

"Can I help you?" said Patrick.

"Well," said the man, his voice shaking, "I....I wanted to talk to you at the funeral, but I just couldn't find the words."

"Yes," said Patrick, "My mother was a wonderful woman. Many will miss her. May I ask how you knew my mother?"

"I'm Blake Ashen. I'm your father."

He just stood there looking at Patrick like he was afraid Patrick was going to rare back and hit him. He really couldn't have blamed Patrick if he did. He knew he deserved it. He had walked out on Victoria and on Patrick before he ever even saw Patrick. He was an alcoholic and a drug addict, and he knew he would be a horrible father.

Patrick was taken aback by the words he had just heard. His father? This man who stood before him with

## No Regrets

his shoulders slouched forward was his father? He wasn't sure how to feel about that. This man had never cared enough about him to stick around, yet here he was now. What did that mean? His father was the first to speak again.

"I know you probably don't want anything to do with me, but I had to see you at least once to apologize for my mistakes. I was a drunk and an addict when I left. I knew you and your mother would be much better off without me. I offer no excuses for my behavior, but I have to at least tell you what happened. Son, I lived on the streets for nearly twenty years. I was in and out of rehab, but as soon as I would get out I would be back on the streets since I had no where to go. Before long I would be right back into my sorry state of existence." Patrick wanted to say something, anything, but he was frozen there, unable to move. Blake continued. "I've been clean for three years now. Every time I would get clean I would start looking for you, but before I knew it I'd be right back to where I started. I knew that I had to stay clean and sober for a while before I could even think about trying to find you. I had come back to Criar because I knew that Victoria's parents had lived here. I thought they might could tell me how to find you. I was sorry to hear they were gone. Of course, that's when I learned that Victoria was living here. I didn't want to interfere with the time you had left with your mother, so I waited. This might not be a good time either." Blake looked down and shuffled his feet with his thumbs stuck in his pockets. He looked as if he expected Patrick to throw him off of the property.

Patrick turned and started walking towards the house. Blake started to turn towards his truck. "Aren't you coming in for a minute?" Patrick said over his shoulder as he continued to walk. Blake stopped, surprised, and hurriedly followed his son into the house.

The girls had already came down from the attic, curious as to who this stranger was. Sarah had gone to the kitchen to make lemonade. It was time for them all to take a break anyway. She had seen the look on Patrick's face as he turned to come in the house, it was tense and unreadable. Who could this stranger be that had taken him from a time of fond memories just moments before? She got the lemonade and carried it to the back deck where they had all sat down. Everyone was quiet, waiting for the stranger to be introduced. The stranger just sat there looking very awkward and out of place.

When everyone was seated and had lemonade before them, the girls turned and waited for Patrick to let them in on the secret of this man. Patrick looked at each of them, still looking dazed. He drew a deep breath and finally spoke.

"Everyone, I'd like for you to meet my father, Blake Ashen."

Eyes flew open wide and Bailey's mouth dropped. She was too young when Blake was around, so she had no remembrance of him. Abigail looked at him with a scrutinizing eye. She was seven when he left, but she really didn't remember that much about him. Sarah carefully watched Patrick, wishing she could read his thoughts. Blake looked like a deer caught in the headlights of a car.

Sarah was first to speak. "Well, Blake, where are you from?"

He fidgeted in his chair and answered. "I'm currently down in San Antonio. I work as a mechanic down there."

The group nodded, not sure where to go with the conversation from there.

"Are you staying here in town?" Sarah continued on.

"Yes," he answered, "I'm over at the Days Inn out by the Interstate."

"How long will you be here?" Bailey asked.

"That just kind of depends. I'll stay around until I can take care of some unfinished business." He looked at his son, who was staring out over the backyard.

They made strained small talk for a little while longer and then Blake stood up to leave.

"I know my visit was a surprise. I truly don't mean to intrude on your time here. I'm in room 47 if you would like to ask me any more questions or just visit some more."

Patrick stood and nodded his acknowledgment. "I'll walk you to your truck," he said.

The two men walked back through the patio door.

The girls' eyes went wide as they looked at each other. What in the world had just happened? They would've been buzzing like little bees had they known what to say. This was certainly an interesting turn of events.

## Chapter 37

Sarah had taken the glasses back into the kitchen and was washing them when Patrick came back in the house. Abigail and Bailey were still on the back deck.

"Are you okay?" she asked.

"I'm not sure," he replied. He walked around to the sink where she stood and before either of them knew it they were embracing. "I'm confused, Sarah," he whispered into her hair. "What am I supposed to think about all of this?"

Her head was reeling from the feelings his embrace was causing. She felt like she should speak some words of wisdom to him right now, but she couldn't. She finally drew in a deep breath and got her mind back on the situation at hand. "You know what you need to do, Patrick."

"I know," he said, "How do I do that? I know I have to forgive him, but I don't know how I'm suppose to take twenty-three years of resentment and just wave them away with my hand."

Sarah took her arms from around him and looked up

at him. She put her hands on his cheeks. "Forgiveness doesn't mean that you automatically forget all the wrongs done to you. It means that you release that person from their guilt. It means that you will never again hold them responsible for the effects of the sin they did against you. It means that you choose to see them through God's eyes and love them as they are." The tears were rolling down Patrick's face as she spoke so gently to him. She wiped the tears away and returned to their embrace. She had resisted this man the whole time she had known him and here she was choosing his most vulnerable time to succumb to her feelings and hold him differently than she ever had before. Had she lost her mind? She was beginning to think that she had.

The back door closing startled both of them and they jumped as they turned to face his sisters. Both of the girls coming in had a questioning look on their face, but they didn't want to jump to any conclusions, although they would not be disappointed if their imagination proved to be right.

Patrick wiped his face and turned to face his sister's stare.

"Are you okay, Patrick?" asked Bailey.

"Yes, I am," he replied. "I'm still very confused, but I know things will work out okay. God will lead me in the decisions I have to make and give me the strength to forgive. This might be a good time to tell you guys something that I haven't even thought of since last Monday." They all looked at him with curiosity. He sighed again, something he had been doing a lot this past week. "Monday morning before I got the call about Mother, I had quit my job and was checking out the colleges for paramedic programs. Mother and I had talked about my dreams that last night. She had told me that I could do anything I wanted. That was another decision I was waiting to tell her when I saw her again." They all stayed quiet, letting Patrick finish and get everything off of his chest. "I quit my job thinking that I would move somewhere closer around here and go to the community college here. The big colleges are just too intimidating. I was trying to follow her wishes for me, but I wasn't ready for big town college life. I haven't thought any more about it, so I'm really not sure what my plans will be when I leave here."

Abigail smiled at her brother. "I'm just proud of you for stepping out in faith, Patrick," she said. "That took a lot of courage. Talk about a new creation. You really took that phrase to heart and reached out to change everything at once."

"That may have seemed like a good idea at the time, Sis, but I'm kind of getting cold feet now." Patrick let out a nervous laugh. "What did I think I was doing? It all seems almost foolish now."

It was Bailey's turn to put in her opinion. "I think that you did make the right decision. If that's what you felt led to do then you just have to trust God that He has a better plan for you. Don't get discouraged. God is trustworthy."

"I sure hope you're right, Sis," he said. "Otherwise I may be coming to live with you."

Bailey was the one to laugh this time, along with the others. "Only if you keep me fed and happy."

He grinned back at her. "That, I can handle. Speaking of which, my stomach is demanding that I feed it before long. How about I fix us some dinner while you finish straightening up the attic? We'll finish going through that stuff tomorrow after we meet with Mr. Duvall."

Mr. Duvall was their mother's attorney and had arranged to come to the house and meet with them tomorrow afternoon. What day was this anyway? They were all starting to blur together. Patrick thought that it was Saturday. They had all planned to stay through next week, finishing up their mother's business. After that, he wasn't sure where he would be.

## Chapter 38

Once again Patrick had cooked a delicious meal and had all of them full and satisfied. There was so much left to go through, but no one was up to continuing tonight. Instead, they spent the evening remembering their mother during her good times. They all had the bad times in the back of their mind, but that's not how they wanted to remember her right now. Sarah excused herself and left the three siblings to themselves. Patrick watched her as she left, remembering the embrace they had shared earlier. He hoped that it was not his imagination that he had felt something there that had never been there before. He had felt an electricity that he had never felt before. He felt very protective of her right now. He knew that she had taken a big loss when his mother died, too. He wanted so badly to hold her and let her know it would be okay.

"Patrick," Bailey said. "Hey, earth to Patrick."

Patrick's mind was aware that his sister was calling him. He just wasn't wanting to leave his thoughts right now. But he knew if he didn't he would be in big trouble. "Yes, sis, I'm still with you." he said as he flashed her one of his charming smiles.

"I was just curious and wanting to know what the

# No Regrets

deal is with you and Sarah." Bailey said.

Abigail broke out laughing, knowing her little sister would be ruthless with him if she didn't get the answer she wanted to hear.

"Excuse me?" Patrick replied, looking like a little boy caught with his hand in the cookie jar.

"I think you heard my question just fine. Now all that is left is for you to answer. Do you think that puppy dog face you had when she left the room went unnoticed?"

"Bailey," he chagrined her, "First of all, who I make puppy dog faces at and what I am thinking is none of your business." He looked so serious for a minute that Bailey was regretting her words, but then he just couldn't hide a smile and she threw a couch pillow at him.

"Watch her, Patrick," Abigail said, "She's a killer with those pillows." It was horrible that it took their mother's death to bring them all closer, but they were each thankful for the new sense of family they had.

"So are you going to answer my question?" Bailey dared to try one more time.

"No," Patrick replied, "There's nothing to tell."

With that he excused himself. He wished he had an answer for them, but the truth was, he didn't. He knew that he saw Sarah as much more than just another pretty face now. He realized the depth of her love for God. She was dedicated to Him with every part of her life. He admired that. He used to think she was prudish, but now he realized what strength it took to be that pure and single minded in this world.

He was headed out to the back deck to sit under the stars for a bit and try to figure out even a part of all the confusion in his mind. As he walked through the kitchen, he spotted Sarah in the sun room. He stood and watched for a little while. She hadn't turned on any lights and the moon was the only light in the room. Its beams touched her golden hair and made her look like an angel. She had her face tilted up and looked like she was having a soothing conversation with a close friend. He knew she was. She was talking to God. He wondered what she was praying about. Was he in her prayers? Was she thinking of him at all? He wanted desperately to go in and talk to her, but he was afraid of distracting her from her time with God. He branded the image of her sitting there on his brain, so that he would never forget it. It was time to walk away from the celestial scene.

He walked out onto the porch and sat in one of the lounge chairs and stared up at the sky that looked like a million twinkling Christmas tree lights.

Sarah loved sitting there in the dark. She would miss this room. It was her haven, her hiding place when things were getting too hard for her to handle. Just being in the living room with Abigail, Bailey, and Patrick was starting to overwhelm her. It was a reminder of her losing them forever in a week. They had talked to her and told her that they wanted to continue to get together and keep in touch with her, but she knew how that usually went. You kept in touch for a while, but eventually the calls and visits would be fewer and further apart. Then you wouldn't hear from them again. How many times had she experienced that? It was hard sitting in that room for another reason, also. Patrick. "Oh, Lord," her heart cried out. "What am I thinking? He's about to leave my world. He's a new Christian. Could he really leave his fast lane world for my world that consists of worshiping You first and foremost? She didn't even know if he was feeling any of the same feelings she was. It was possible that the feeling she felt when he hugged her today was totally one sided.

She spotted him now, out on the deck. He was lying in the same lounge chair that his mother had just a week ago when they had their cookout. "I miss you so much, Ms. Victoria," she whispered as she turned her face up toward heaven. She would love to go talk to him, but what if he wanted to be alone. She wouldn't intrude. He seemed lost in his thoughts and he had a lot to think about with his father. She had no business adding to his confusion right now. She watched him for a few more minutes. His lips were moving as he looked upward. She couldn't be more proud that he had given his life to Christ. He seemed to be plunging in head first and not looking back. That sent a tingle up her spine. "Enough of this teenage dreaming. There's so much still left to do tomorrow," she chided herself. She tidied up the kitchen and retired to the bedroom that had come to feel like it was meant to be hers, like she belonged here.

When Patrick came back inside he had hoped that Sarah might still be in the sun room, that he might happen to run into her before she went to bed, but the house was dark. He went around checking the windows and doors and headed up the stairs to his own room. He smiled when he heard his sister's talking quietly as he passed by their room. By the time he got ready for bed and read a little of his Bible, the stress of the day was beginning to catch up with him. He whispered a little prayer before drifting off, "God, if I am to forgive my father, You're going to have to be the One to provide the strength to do that."

## Chapter 39

They had decided not to get into much cleaning today. It was Sunday and they didn't feel like they could face the crowds at church today, so they decided it would be best to enjoy their day together and relax. Their mother's attorney was coming by after he got home from church and ate lunch, so that would fill their afternoon.

Abigail had decided she would work in the garden for a while. It had been neglected of late and there were flowers blooming everywhere, almost taking over. She pruned back bushes and plants making sure she filled every vase she could possibly find with the excess flowers. The house was permeated with the smell of Spring. She wished she had done this the past few weeks, but she hadn't and she couldn't go back in time. They had all agreed to a pact of no regrets. The past is just that, the past. There's nothing any of them could say or do to change that. They had all forgiven each other for whatever haunted their minds and that was that. They would only look forward to the future now.

Bailey and Patrick had gone down the road to a

pond they used to fish at quite a bit. This was nice. The two of them hadn't had much time to themselves and they wanted to make sure they took advantage of the time they now shared. Bailey relentlessly teased him about Sarah. Patrick was, for the most part, just very evasive, but suddenly stopped and confided in his sister. "Bailey, I used to look at Sarah with just the desire and passion that I saw any attractive girl with, but since I became a Christian it's different."

"Different in what way?" Bailey said, surprised that he had shared that with her.

He hesitated for a moment and then turned those gorgeous eyes of his and fixed them on his sister. "I really care about protecting her from guys like I used to be. I see her now as she is, always has been, I just hadn't known it then. She's God's child, Bailey. How could I have ever had any other intentions towards her like I did? In fact, I'm quite ashamed of how I've treated the women in my life. I haven't given them the respect that they deserved. I only cared about what I wanted or what they could do for me." Bailey sat there for a moment, silent. A tear rolled down her cheek. "What did I say wrong?" Patrick said, trying to recount his words.

Bailey was shaking her head and wiping the tears. "No," she said, laughing, "You didn't say anything wrong."

"Then why are you crying?" Patrick said, confused.

"Because," Bailey replied, "you have just said one of the most romantic things I have ever heard."

"Romantic?" Patrick said, his eyebrows burrowed.

"Yes," said Bailey, "to honor a woman like that with a godly respect is the highest form of romance in my book. Do you know how much I long to meet someone who thinks that way towards me?"

"The men better treat you with respect or they'll have to deal with me." Patrick said, smiling and nudging his sister. "Come on," he said, "We better get back to the house."

They gathered up their poles and tackle boxes, released the two small fish they had caught back into the pond and started back towards the house.

Sarah spent the morning going to town and getting groceries. She had volunteered to cook lunch for everyone to give Patrick a break. She didn't exactly have the gourmet flare that Patrick had, but no one would shy away from her meals. Her grandmother had taught her a thing or two about good old southern cooking when she was a teen.

Sarah had also spent a lot of time that morning thinking about changing jobs. This job was heart wrenching and it might be time to check out the small local hospital and see if they had any openings. She loved taking care of people in the manner she had been, but not only was it hard on the heart in the end, but it didn't free up much time for a social life. Sarah had never been one to do much socially, but it would be nice to at least make a couple of friends her own age, have someone to go out to eat with or to a movie. She had never really even had a desire for that before meeting Victoria's family. There was just something special about Abigail, Bailey, and Patrick. She longed to spend more time with them. Tomorrow, she promised herself, she would start moving towards a new life.

## Chapter 40

With lunch over and the kitchen cleaned they all went into the living room to chat for a bit before Mr. Duvall arrived to go over their mother's estate with them. They didn't have much time to chat; he drove up just minutes after they got settled in their chairs. Sarah went to greet Mr. Duvall and usher him into the living room. She was backing out through the door to give them privacy when Mr. Duvall addressed her.

"No, Sarah, you need to stay as well."

Sarah had a look of surprise on her face, but walked back to the chair she had occupied earlier and quietly clasped her hands in her lap and kept her eyes averted down, feeling like an intruder. Abigail noticed how uncomfortable Sarah was and reached across the end table that separated them, motioning for Sarah to give her hand, which Sarah complied.

"Sarah," Abigail said, "You are a part of this family, as far as I'm concerned. You belong here."

Sarah smiled. She had never really belonged to a family. It was always just her and her grandmother. She looked across the room and Bailey had the sweetest look on her face that mirrored Abigail's sentiments. She wasn't sure what she saw in Patrick's eyes. It was a warm look with just a hint of longing. She felt her cheeks flush and looked back down at her lap.

Mr. Duvall had settled on the couch and had taken out a manila folder with what looked to be their mother's will. He sat still for a minute to gain his professional composure and then looked at each person in the room. He spent a few minutes telling the children how and when he had first met their mother. He shared funny little stories from past times and made sure they knew that their mother was not just a client, she was his friend. Apparently their mother had even sat for hours on end with his wife when she went through her bout with cancer. The respect he had for their mother was evident in his face. When he finished his sentiments, he pulled his glasses from his inside coat pocket and held the papers out to where he could read them.

He looked at Sarah first. "Sarah," he said, "Victoria grew to love you very quickly. You were more than just her nurse. She thought of you as one of her own. She wanted you to have the emerald ring that you admired on many occasions." Sarah's eyes widened as she listened to him continue. "She also wanted you to have her car. She had just bought it right before she became sick. She wanted you to have good solid transportation, unlike the, as she put it, 'heap of metal' you drive now."

That brought strains of laughter from everyone in the room. Sarah tried to feign offense, but she was far from offended. She was overwhelmed. She had known and loved this lady for fourteen months and she was willing to share these expensive and personal things with

# No Regrets

her? Sarah was not used to that kind of love in her life. She didn't know whether to laugh or cry, so she did both. She panicked for a minute and wondered if the others would be upset because their mother had left her these things, but the look on their faces dispelled that thought quickly.

When things settled back down, Mr. Duvall looked down at the paper again and read quietly for just a moment. He then looked at Abigail and Bailey.

"Girls," he started, "your mother wants you to divide all of her remaining jewelry." Both girls nodded as he continued. "Abigail, your mother would like for you to have the china that had been her mother's. Bailey, you are to have the silver tea set. She also told me to make sure that you knew you would be expected to have lots of tea parties and to make sure that Abigail attended and 'had fun'."

They all laughed quietly. Even after she was gone their mother was trying to add humor to the situation to make them smile.

"There is also a life insurance policy that will be divided three ways. I have those checks with me today and will take care of getting those dispersed before I leave."

Heads were still nodding slowly and somberly. So this is what they were being paid off with in exchange for their mother. Any one of them would give them back and everything they owned to have their mother back. Mr. Duvall turned to his right to face Patrick, who was sitting beside him.

Patrick said, "Don't tell me, I get the silverware, right?"

With a chuckle, Mr. Duvall said, "Well, I don't have that written down here, so that will have to be between you and your sisters." Abigail shot him a glance with her eyebrows raised. "But I will tell you what your mother has left for you," he continued. "Your mother had set up college funds for each of you when you were born. They didn't amount to very much, but before your grandmother and grandfather passed they had set up college funds for you as well. As you know, your sisters have depleted their college funds. It was your mother's wish that you use yours, as well."

Patrick was fighting back the tears. How did his mother know he would be wanting to go to college and make something of himself. He had about given that dream up this past week. He didn't know how he would do it without his mother's encouragement.

"That's not all, Patrick," he continued, "She also left you the house. She wasn't sure how you'd feel about living here, but thought maybe you could keep it up for the three of you to get together or something of that nature."

Patrick wasn't believing his ears. She left *him* the house? He was the youngest. Why would she do that?

"It's okay, Patrick," Bailey said, "Get that look off of your face. Mother had talked to both Abigail and me when she was making these decisions. We thought it was a wonderful idea."

Patrick just put his head in his hands. Was this what they meant by God's blessings? He had done nothing to deserve any blessings. His dad came to the forefront of his mind. It's not about deserving blessings, it's about mercy and grace. He knew now what he had to do, and what further amazed him was that he wanted to do it. He would make the call right after they were finished here.

Mr. Duvall asked if any of them had any questions,

to which he received heads nodding no, each lost in their own thoughts. "If you have no questions," he said, standing, "I'll leave these checks with you. I'll have paperwork ready to sign for the house and car and such in a couple of days. I'll call you to let you know when I'll be coming back out."

Abigail stood and walked Mr. Duvall to the front door. "Thank you, Mr. Duvall," Abigail said, "Not just for what you've done here today, but for being a friend to our mother. We appreciate that immensely."

"The pleasure was definitely all mine," he replied and then turned and walked down the steps out to his car.

Abigail stood leaning against the porch railing and watched until his car disappeared behind the row of pine trees that lined the front part of the property.

Patrick stood and bolted out of the room. Bailey and Sarah exchanged glances, but both stayed seated. Patrick bounded up the stairs and went to his room to retrieve the number to Days Inn off of his dresser. He used the upstairs phone and made his phone call short and sweet. At least he hoped he hadn't sounded harsh. "God, it's all up to You now." He said looking upward.

They cooked out again that evening, but it just wasn't as joyful a time as it had been the week before. The lounge chair was painfully empty. They still had a wonderful time just sitting out under the stars. Patrick asked his sisters their opinion of him going to the junior college here in Criar. He really wanted their input and prayers. He wanted all the major decisions in his life to be prayed over from now on, no more making a mess of his life. They thought it was a wonderful idea and promised that they would come down at least once a month to have family time. Sarah felt a strange presence of excitement knowing that he was going to be in the same town as her now. They talked late into the night, knowing that they had things to take care of tomorrow, but nothing pressing. It would all get done in time.

Abigail started gathering up the remains of the dishes outside.

"Bailey, will you help me clean up? Sarah and Patrick have done most of the cooking, it's our time to pitch in."

"Sure," Bailey said, all too aware of what her sister was thinking.

When the door closed Patrick let out a little laugh. "Why do I feel like that was a planned conspiracy?" Sarah wasn't sure if he was pleased with the situation or not. She felt her face grow hot in the dark. "Patrick, please don't feel like you have to stay out here unless you want to. I think I am going to stay out a little longer."

Patrick stood up and slid his chair over beside Sarah. "Are you kidding?" he said, "I've been waiting for this opportunity for days."

She really felt flushed now. She turned to look at him, the moon just made his smile that much brighter. She ducked her head and smiled and felt his hand on her own. She had never really had anyone she seriously liked in her life, so this was intoxicating and a little scary. After all, he had dated lots of women who were probably prettier and more exciting than her.

He took her hand and enclosed it between both of his. "Sarah, I want you to know something. I realize what a precious and rare gem you are. You are truly a woman of God and I am in awe at your wisdom and your dedication to Him. I respect you, Sarah. I want to get to know you better. I know my life hasn't been anywhere equal to yours in the God department, but I do want to change that. I'm falling in love with Him more and more every day." Sarah went to say something and he placed his finger to her lips, noticing how soft they were. "I'm sorry that I have been in the world all these years. Not only for myself, but for the woman I'll marry someday. I can never again be *innocent*, but I want God to purify my heart and mind and body so that I can someday give myself wholly to my wife. I have no idea what the future might hold for us, Sarah, but as long as you are a part of my life in some way, I will feel very blessed."

The tears were spilling over from the pools in her eyes. He took the same finger that he had placed on her lips just minutes before and wiped away her tears. He wanted so badly to take her in his arms and kiss her, but he didn't. It wasn't the right time. So he leaned over as he rose from his chair and gave her a gentle kiss on the cheek, letting his lips linger there for just a few more seconds. Sarah had to remind herself to breath as she watched him walk inside.

When he had disappeared inside Abigail and Bailey came busting through the sliding glass door looking like giggling teenage girls.

Bailey plopped down in the seat her brother had just vacated and leaned over with wide eyes to Sarah. "I don't know what all he just said to you, but I can tell by that look on your face that you need to stay in our room tonight. We have a lot to talk about."

## Chapter 41

Patrick didn't even want to know what had gone on in the room next to him last night. He had still heard laughter at 4:00 a.m. when he got up to go to the bathroom. Whatever it was, he hoped their laughter was a good sign, and they weren't laughing at him. The look on the girl's faces as they came dragging into the kitchen said they would pay for their late night escapades today. He just shook his head and smiled as he poured them each a cup of coffee. He couldn't help but notice how Sarah looked like she was becoming one of them more and more every day.

"Not a word, baby brother," Abigail growled in his direction.

He held up his hands in surrender. "I didn't say a word."

They all looked somewhat revived after the mouth watering western omelets that Patrick had made them. Where did that boy learn to do that? They were still dragging a little, though, as they drifted off in a daze to get dressed. Sarah had planned to go to the hospital this morning and check into job openings. She would love to take the car Victoria had given her, but almost felt guilty, which was silly because she had driven it almost daily while Victoria was still alive. She needed to decide what to do with hers. She would donate it to the women's shelter, but she was afraid it was in too bad of shape. Maybe she could talk to Pastor Tim and see if there were men in the church that might could work on it and get it in decent shape for the shelter. She would stop by the church and talk to him on her way home.

Abigail and Bailey planned to continue going through the things in the attic today. Since they would be down here visiting Patrick monthly, time was not of the essence, but they still wanted to clean out some things. They would go through their mother's clothes and personal things today and decide what the shelter could use. They knew that Patrick would probably want to take the larger master bedroom since it was his house now, but they didn't want him to feel like he was invading their mother's space. They would help him clean it out this week and maybe buy him a new comforter set or something to make it feel a little less feminine and a little more like his space instead of his mother's. They knew that unless they took the initiative that he would leave everything exactly as it was now. They didn't want him feeling like he needed to do that. This was a new beginning for him and they were so proud of the changes they had seen just within a week.

Patrick wanted to mow the yard and clean up a little around the outside of the house today, but not until after his visitor came and went. Right now he wanted to find a quiet place and spend some time with God. He needed all the strength and wisdom he could get today. What happened if the hurt and bitterness came pouring out instead of mercy and grace? No. He wouldn't let that happen. If God could forgive him, he could forgive the man who walked out on him twenty-three years ago. He went to the den and shut the door behind him. He could almost still feel his mother's presence here. He chose the chair over by the window. There was a great view from this window of the small patch of woods that separated their land from the neighbors. It brought him such comfort to know that he could stay here. He couldn't imagine anyone else ever coming into this house besides them. It was the only place his mother had ever really called home and he would love and protect this home now.

    He didn't really know where to start in this conversation with God. His emotions were conflicting and warring within him. He had read in Luke that God knew everything about him, so he decided it best to just get everything out on the table. He told God everything he was feeling, the good, along with the bad. He poured out his heart until he was emptied of words and tears. Then he listened. He listened for that still small voice that would give him direction. There it was. He could feel it pouring over him like warm oil. He felt the peace and the comfort, and he knew, once again, that this was what his mother had talked about when she talked about sitting in God's lap and letting Him hold you. He didn't want to let go of this feeling. He had never felt so safe and secure before in his life. How could he have been so blind, causing him to miss out on so many years that could've been spent right here in God's arms? It was time to leave the private and personal time he was enjoying alone with God for now. His father was driving up the drive way.

## Chapter 42

Blake Ashen had spent the past forty-eight hours on pins and needles. He couldn't believe he had actually stood face to face with his son. He had almost given up hope of him calling, and then almost ran out of the room in fear when his son finally did call. He wasn't sure what would happen today between him and his son. Patrick's voice was so void of any emotion when he called that Blake had no idea if Patrick was going to tell him off and throw him out on his ear or what. He knew he didn't deserve Patrick's forgiveness, but he couldn't live another day without at least asking for it. He also didn't want his son to live with bitterness in his heart. He wanted to release him of that. Blake had spent most of his life living with bitterness and resentment and he knew just how bad it could eat away at your heart. Had the counselor at rehab not led him to Christ, the bitterness and resentment and hate probably would've killed him. He would've either drank himself to death or killed himself with the drugs just trying to cover up the pain he felt. Here he was now, driving up the drive way to what might be the last time he would ever see his son.

God knew his heart and knew how much he wanted this to be a beginning, not an end, but he would accept whatever came. He had learned long ago that you have to accept the consequences of your sins.

Blake was shaking as he stepped out of the truck. There he was, his son, standing on the porch. He had never expected him to be so tall and handsome. He most certainly got his looks from Victoria. Patrick was now bounding down the front steps, coming out to meet him.

When the two met in the middle Patrick's only words were, "Let's take a walk."

With that Patrick turned and started walking. Blake just knew that those words were sealing his fate with his son. He was now expecting him to say that he didn't want anything to do with him and to leave his life forever. Blake hung his head and stuck his hands in his pockets and followed the son that he regretted leaving behind for so many years.

Patrick led him to the patch of woods that served as a divider between properties. They climbed over dead trees that had fallen and through berry vines that clung to their pant legs. They finally came to a spot that made Blake's eyes widened. It was beautiful here. The huge moss rocks that seemed to liter the woods were abundant here and shaded by huge oak and maple trees.

"Have a seat," Patrick said, pointing to a huge flat rock. "I found this place when we first moved here. It's where I came to be alone, mostly to get away from the girls." He smiled at the memory.

"It's beautiful here." Blake said, still cautious with his son.

Patrick took a seat on another rock about three feet away. He sat there with one leg hiked up on the rock with his arm resting on top of his knee. He was looking up, deep in thought and Blake almost felt as if Patrick had forgotten he was there. Blake just sat silently, waiting for his judgment to be handed down.

After what seemed like forever, Patrick took a deep breath and let it out slowly and then turned and faced his father.

"Dad," the very word pierced Blake's heart, "I forgive you."

Blake was blinking rapidly trying to keep the tears from falling, but to no avail. They flowed freely as Blake's body began to shake. He put his head in his hands and cried. He thanked God that he had been given redemption. Blake knew he had received it from God, but he needed it from Patrick.

"Thank you, son," Blake said, "I know I don't deserve your forgiveness."

Patrick moved over to a rock closer to his dad. "Dad, none of us deserve forgiveness, that's what grace is for. I've only come to learn that for myself this past week. I wish I had listened to my mother and sisters long ago when they tried to explain it to me."

Blake knew he could not be more proud of his son than he was at this moment. Oh, the sorrow that he felt for the missed time. "Son," he said, "I just want you to know how much I regret my decisions in life."

"No, dad," Patrick said, shaking his head, "No regrets. The paths that we took along the way have led us here to this moment and have taught us about God's mercy and grace. I don't want to you regret your life. Let go of the past and let's look forward to the future."

"I'm so sorry about your mother," Blake said, looking down at the ground. "I owe her all my gratitude for raising you up to be the fine man I see you've become."

Patrick laughed, "Believe me, she had quite a job keeping up with me, but I'm thankful she never gave up. One of these days I'll tell you a story of just how awesome my mother was." Patrick stood and placed his hand on his father's shoulder. "Let's go, dad, it's time to begin a new life together."

The two men were quiet on the walk back to the house. There was so much each wanted to ask the other, but there would be time for that.

Blake stayed for another hour or so enjoying lemonade that Sarah had brought out to them. Patrick had invited his sisters and Sarah to sit and visit with them. Bailey asked most of the questions. She never was one to be shy. Blake hated to leave, but he knew he had to get back on the road. He wanted to know everything there was about his son and take every advantage of this second chance at fatherhood. They made plans to get together again in a few weeks. His father would come back out to the house and stay for a few days. They would have no distractions and could truly be reunited.

## Chapter 43

Patrick went out on the back deck where Sarah was sitting in a lounge chair after dinner. She smiled up at him.

"Are you okay?" She said.

"I think so," he replied. "I'm just so overwhelmed at where my life has gone in such a short period of time. Two weeks ago I was only interested in hitting the bars. That life seems so far away now."

"Do you miss it?" She said. He looked pensive for a moment and then looked down at her and smiled.

"Not at all." He held out his hand to her. "Let's take a walk." She reached up and took his and let him help her up.

Abigail called Bailey to the kitchen window. They stood there smiling as they watched the two walk off hand in hand. They had come to love Sarah and wouldn't mind one bit if she would someday become a permanent part of their family.

"Where do you think your next job will take you?" Patrick said, looking off in the distance as they walked.

"Well, I have an interview next Monday at the hospital in town. If that works out I'll be staying right here."

Patrick stopped and took her by the shoulders. "Do you think I might could take you out sometime?" Sarah raised her eyes to meet his.

"I'd be disappointed if you didn't."

His eyes sparkled and he took her face in his hands. He couldn't resist leaning down and touching her lips with his. It would crush him if she pulled away, but his fear of that was soon dispelled. Sarah returned his kiss and felt feelings she didn't think she had ever felt before. Could it be love she was feeling? His kiss was gentle. He was horrified that he might have offended her in some way when she pulled away just a bit.

"Oh, Patrick," she said.

"I'm sorry, Sarah, I didn't mean to offend you."

"No, that wasn't what I meant," she whispered as she wrapped her arms around him and held him tightly.

They spent the rest of the evening walking and talking and holding hands. It was if they were afraid the other would float up into the air and disappear if they let go. By the time they returned to the house it was almost dark. They were starving, but figured the girls hadn't waited for them to get back. When they went through the back door they were met by Abigail and Bailey who were standing there with their arms crossed feigning irritation.

"Sorry we're late," Patrick said, "Have you eaten yet?"

"Well, we would've liked to have eaten by now," Bailey said. "We worked hard all afternoon preparing supper and now it's cold."

"Wait," said Patrick. "You two cooked?"

# No Regrets

The sisters looked at each other, looking very insulted. "We drove all the way into town to pick up the pizza!" Abigail yelled out.

With that the two girls busted out with laughter. They ran around the bar and gave Sarah and Patrick a hug.

"Does this mean that we'll still be seeing you regularly, Sarah?"

"Bailey!" said Abigail as she swatted at her sister with her hand. "You are way too blunt and nosey."

"Oh, please, sister, dear," replied Bailey. "You know you're wanting to know that as much as I am."

Patrick reached for Sarah and rescued her from his two sisters. "Would you two leave the poor girl alone? We haven't even gone out on a date yet." Patrick said, standing behind Sarah with his arms protectively around her shoulders.

Sarah just stood there grinning from ear to ear. She had never had this many people wanting her around. It felt good. It felt like family.

## Chapter 44

The rest of the week went by way too fast for any of their likings. All three girls were like mother hens trying to clean out the house, trying to get it to feel a little bit more like home for Patrick. They would clean out something they thought should be changed and then would all head to the mall in the next town over and buy stuff to replace it. The sisters made sure they paid attention to what drew Sarah's eye, too. Then they would lean in that direction. Who knew what might happen in the future.

Patrick talked to his dad a few times throughout the week. It felt strange to all of a sudden have him in his life, but it was a good kind of strange. He had also gone to the community college there close by and talked to a counselor who helped him line out his course of action for becoming a paramedic. He knew that if he had been alone in this he never could've taken on that much work. He would have given up. But with the new closeness he had with his sisters and with Sarah's encouragement, he knew there was no way they would let him not succeed. Sarah. His heart fluttered every time he saw her or just thought about her. Somehow he knew he'd marry that girl someday.

The four would spend their evenings sitting on the porch or in the den talking about Victoria and remembering the mother they had just come to understand. Looking back, she had been a wonderful mother. She sacrificed so much of herself to try to make things half-way normal for them. They had nothing but gratitude and respect for her and they would be sure to remember the good times and honor their mother.

The last evening before Abigail and Bailey went back to their lives and Sarah would move into her apartment in town, the three siblings handed a small package to Sarah.

"What's this?" Sarah said, her shyness causing red to creep into her cheeks.

"It's something of our mother's that we would like for you to have," said Abigail.

Sarah took the package in her hands and slowly began to unwrap the package. Tears came to her eyes when she saw Victoria's Bible that she had used the most. Sarah had loved to flip through the pages of that Bible and read all of the notes Victoria had made.

"Are you sure?" she said with a quivering voice.

"Yes," said Bailey. "We couldn't think of anyone else who would treasure it more."

The tears gently rolled down Sarah's face as each one gave her a hug.

They were having a cookout to commemorate their last night together. There was plenty of laughter and food to go around. Bailey had the music blaring, as usual. Abigail stopped cold in her tracks when she heard the familiar voice of LeeAnn Womack. There was the song, *I Hope You Dance*. The memories of her mother's words to her came flooding back to her now as she closed her eyes and listened. No one else had noticed the song that now filled more than her ears, but also her soul. She walked down the back steps of the deck and began to twirl and dance to the music like never before. Sarah was the first to notice and touched Patrick's arm and nodded towards the yard. Bailey saw the gesture as well and they all stood there watching Abigail as her soul took flight from the darkness that had entrapped her for so many years. When the song was over Abigail sat right down where she stood in the grass. She was breathing hard, but could never remember a moment where she felt more free.

# Chapter 45

They had stayed outside talking and visiting until almost midnight. Tomorrow was going to be hard for them. Not only did they not want to leave each other, but it would feel like they were finally saying goodbye to Victoria. They planned on going to the cemetery tomorrow morning and then go their separate ways after lunch.

Abigail's cheeks hurt from smiling so much tonight. She went back over every detail of the evening as she stepped into the shower. The steaming hot water felt so good as she let it hit the back of her neck. She turned and let it hit her full in the face. It was hot, but it felt good. She had taken the soap and began bathing when she froze where she was. The water may have been hot, but she had chills on her body. She felt again. Had that been there before? She had never noticed it if it had. She shook her head. No. It was her imagination. Why wouldn't she be paranoid after just losing her mother to breast cancer? She vowed to put it out of her mind, but the vow didn't last long. She couldn't help but to feel one more time. There was definitely something there. It didn't necessarily mean cancer though, right? Abigail began to shake again. She slid down the wall of the shower until she reached the ceramic tile floor. Her sobs came hard now. She buried her face in her hands trying to muffle the sobs that she could no longer control. "Why, God?" she cried out. "Please, God, I can't handle this. Don't do this to me and my family. It's too much!"

Bailey had gone back up to their room to get a light jacket. All but Abigail were still lingering outside. She was walking out whistling when she thought she heard something. She stopped and listened. She knocked on the door of the bathroom across the hall where Abigail was taking a shower.

"Everything okay, sis?" Bailey listened for a reply but heard nothing. "Abigail?" She tried again. Nothing. Maybe she just can't hear over the water," Bailey thought to herself. She was starting to walk away when she thought she heard a moan. She stepped back and listened again. She heard what sounded like another moan. She opened the door just a crack. "Abigail?" she said softly. She looked towards the frosted glass door of the shower, half expecting to be embarrassed from barging in on her sister, but instead all she saw was a dark figure huddled in the floor of the shower. "Abigail?" she said again, slowly making her way towards the shower. She could hear the sobs now that were muffled from somewhere deep within the shower stall. She opened the shower door just a crack. "Abigail, what is it?" Abigail didn't answered, but just continued to sob. Bailey thought about turning off the water, but it was still hot and she didn't want her sister sitting there shivering, so she just let it continue to run over her. Bailey opened the door completely and kneeled down beside the edge of the

## No Regrets

shower stall. "Abigail, you have to talk to me," she said, reaching out to touch her sister's arm. Abigail was shaking horribly as she slowly lifted her head and met her sister's gaze. Bailey was so scared for a minute. The look on Abigail's face was completely blank. "Abby, don't do this to me. Please talk to me."

Abigail's voice was low and hoarse when she finally spoke. "I found a knot in my breast."

Bailey flinched, but kept her composure. "Are you sure? Maybe it's just something you haven't noticed before." Bailey was trying really hard to be positive here and not panic.

Abigail looked up at her sister and said, "Bailey, you know both of us were trained how to correctly check our breast when mother was diagnosed, and you have checked yourself as much as I have. It's there."

Bailey just stared blankly at her sister. The tears were still rolling down Abigail's cheeks, mingled with the waterfall from the shower head. Bailey's eyes began to flood with tears. She crawled in the shower, not caring that she was still dressed, and took her sister in her arms and sat there and rocked her back and forth.

"I won't let anything happen to you," Bailey promised. "I'll go home with you and we'll call the doctor tomorrow for an appointment and we'll stop it as soon as we can. We can do this, Abigail. I just found my sister, my friend, I won't lose you." Bailey continued to say anything positive that she could think of, but in her mind she was shaking her fist at God.

They stayed in the floor of the shower until the water ran cold. Bailey reached up and turned the water off. She got out and got a towel for her sister. She helped her out of the floor and wrapped her in the towel. Abigail just sat down staring into space as Bailey removed her wet clothes and dried off as well.

"I wonder what is taking Bailey so long?" said Patrick.

"Knowing your sister," said Sarah, "she got sidetracked and forgot all about us or got up there and started another pillow fight with Abigail."

"You're probably right," replied Patrick.

"Are you complaining?" teased Sarah.

"Not at all!" exclaimed Patrick. He reached over and took Sarah's hand. He stared at her profile in the moonlight. In his opinion he had never seen anyone as beautiful as this precious woman who was sitting here holding his hand.

Bailey cleaned up the water on the floor and got her sister situated on the bed in their bedroom. She got Abigail dressed in a fresh gown and got her to lay down. Bailey then got changed herself and then went and sat on the side of Abigail's bed. Abigail put her head in her younger sister's lap and for the first time ever let Bailey take care of her.

"I don't want anyone to know," whispered Abigail.

"I agree," said Bailey, "because when we get to the doctor we're going to find out that it's nothing serious, just a cyst or something."

They both wanted to believe this so badly.

"You're going to see, Abby, it's all going to be okay," Bailey cooed as she stroked her sister's hair. Bailey stayed right beside Abigail the entire night.

## Chapter 46

Breakfast was very subdued that next morning. Abigail and Bailey had agreed that they would go home as they had planned so that Bailey could check in with her work and plan on a short leave of absence and get some things she needed from her apartment. Patrick just assumed the quietness stemmed from the departures that were coming too quickly. He never imagined that he would miss his sister's like he knew he would when they left today. He would help Sarah move into her new apartment this afternoon when she returned from her interview. The interview was pretty much a formality, but was part of the red tape that would have to be gone through for her to start at the hospital. Sarah didn't have much to move, but the girls had insisted that she take the furniture that they were replacing with more manly furniture for Patrick, along with any of the bedding and accessories that they replaced. Patrick wanted her to take the couch from the den until she could get one of her own. If he had his way she would only use it until he could convince her to marry him, but he didn't want to scare her, so he kept that to himself.

They went to the cemetery that morning and took fresh flowers to their mother's grave site. The grave stone had been put in place since they had been here for the funeral. They had chosen a pink granite stone with her name and dates of birth and death. Across the bottom there were two simple words. *No Regrets.* They could think of no better tribute to their mother's life. She had lived the best she knew how and had served God with all her heart. Whether her life had turned out perfect made no difference, only that she had a desire and will to follow God. Isn't that all He asks of us? There's no way to control all of the courses of our life. All we can do is trust God and let Him be in control. No matter where that leads us, we just have to keep trusting.

Abigail and Bailey held hands standing there over their mother's grave. Seeing their mother's grave stone and discussing what those two words meant gave them a peace and a hope that all would work out. They would trust God. They would trust that He had brought them all closer together for a reason, and there was a reason for whatever would happen next. After all, God's word promises that all things work for the good of those who love the Lord. They would cling to this promise.

After lunch the two girls packed their cars and headed for home. They were reluctant to leave Patrick and Sarah behind, but they were anxious to get back to the city to get things taken care of with Abigail.

Patrick had never gotten around to mowing the lawn Saturday, so he took this opportunity to take care of that. It helped get his mind off of the empty house. It was strange knowing that this house was his now. It seemed so big now that everyone was gone. He would have to go back to his apartment in the city to clear out his stuff one day this week. There wasn't much to get, but he would rent a U-Haul when he got home. Wait, he *was* home. When he got to the city, he corrected himself. He could get a couple of friends to help him load everything that night and could head back first thing the next morning. He didn't want to spend any more time away from Sarah then he had to. He wasn't really sure how this dating God's way would go, but she was sure worth finding out. These feelings were new to him, but welcomed.

When Sarah returned from her interview, now an employee of the hospital, they began taking truck loads to her new apartment. It only took three trips since she didn't have much. The apartment was bare, but she knew she could get a few things, little by little, to make it feel more like home.

When they finished, they went to a restaurant in town to get something to eat. Not exactly the first date Patrick had in mind, but there would be time for that. He took her back to her apartment and hated having to say goodnight. They had talked while they moved today and set boundaries for their private times together so that they wouldn't get themselves into a compromising situation. That was really a change for Patrick. He had never even thought about boundaries before, but he wanted with all his heart to protect Sarah from anything that would cause her to stray from God or that would hurt her. He walked her up to her apartment and gave her a long hug. He wanted to remember the scent of her hair, the way she fit just right in his arms. He looked down at her and kissed her forehead. This was going to be tougher than he thought. "God, I'm going to need Your strength in this, too," he silently prayed. He was realizing just how much he was going to need God's strength in all areas of his life.

    He walked into the big house that was now dark and quiet. It had been a long day. Time to get some sleep in the new room the girls had made him. It didn't seem right, but he had to make the change sometime. It might as well be now.

## Chapter 47

Bailey got pulled over by a Highway Patrolman on the way home. He was a young guy and it didn't take much to sweet talk him into giving her a warning. She hadn't meant to speed, but her mind was on her sister. She was in a hurry to get back to the city and take care of her business and go meet Abigail. She took advantage of her cell phone on the way home and called the office and talked to her boss. She arranged to be on a leave of absence until her sister was seen to and taken care of.

Abigail took her time driving home. She knew she needed to get back in time to call the doctor's office, but she felt a dread wash over her. Maybe if she just ignored it, it would go away. She knew better than to play with her life like that, she just didn't want to have to face anything else right now. Despite the loss of her mother, Abigail had felt lighter in soul than she had ever remembered. This couldn't really be happening, could it? Surely, the doctor would say she was being silly and that her imagination was playing with her emotions that had been so vulnerable lately. She had talked to Dave at the office yesterday and told him she would be delayed a little longer in coming back. She didn't want to have to deal with everyone making a fuss over her when she didn't even know if there was anything to fuss over. She would get home, call the doctor, unpack and then take a long hot bubble bath and listen to some classical music. That was the best stress reliever she had found over the years. There was something about the soft whine of a cello that allowed her mind to drift away to unknown worlds. Candles. She couldn't forget the candles.

Bailey walked into her apartment and went through the huge stack of mail that her neighbor had been picking up for her. Most of it was junk mail, a few were bills. She would need to write those out and send them off before she left. She would hate to come home to an apartment with no electricity or water. She walked by the stereo on the way to the bedroom and pushed the on button. The loud, steady rhythm of the music had her bopping to the beat the whole time she unpacked and packed yet again. She loved music that she could prance around the room to while singing into her hair brush. Bailey couldn't sing a lick, but she could lip sync better than any rock star she knew. She put her bags by the door and sat down to write the bills out. She could drop these by the post office a couple of blocks away on the way out. She checked and made sure everything was off, then with one last look around the apartment that she was beginning to miss, she turned off the lights, locked the door, and headed out again. The drive to Abigail's would normally take about an hour and a half, but if she hit rush hour she'd be at least two and a half hours.

When Abigail walked into her apartment her cat, JoJo jumped out at her, scaring her to death. She had

## No Regrets

expected him to be mad at her, though. He usually was when she left him for very long. He would pout and stalk around tonight, but would forgive her by morning. She would have loved to sit down for a while before unpacking or going through mail or answering phone messages, but there was something she had to do first. She got her address book and looked up the name of her doctor. He knew the history of her mother and had always worked well with her if she ever had any questions or wanted him to check something she thought she felt. He was very cautious and excellent at calming her fears. She hoped he could do that this time. She talked to the nurse and told her the situation. The nurse said she would tell Dr. Adams and get back to her as soon as she could. Abigail would use the waiting time for unpacking. She needed her mind to be busy. She had barely got unpacked when the phone rang. It was the nurse. She had talked to Dr. Adams and he had set her up for a mammogram the next day at two o'clock. He had sent word for her to not worry, that it was probably just another false alarm, but they would check and make sure for good measure. "See," she told herself, "nothing to worry about." She took care of her mail, answered a few phone messages that could be answered quickly and then headed to her haven of bubbles and candles and orchestras lulling her into a deep relaxation. She had told Bailey she would wait for her to get there before eating and they could go out and get something together. They needed to keep busy tonight. There would be time to think about things when they found out if there was anything to even think about.

The traffic wasn't as bad as Bailey had feared it would be on her way to Abigail's apartment. There had been an accident on I-30, but she saw the traffic stalled far enough ahead that she was able to get off on the service road and make a slight detour to get around it much quicker than the ones still sitting still, waiting for the cars to be moved off of the road. She couldn't wait to get to Abigail's. She was starving. She didn't know what Abigail wanted, but her mouth was watering for a club sandwich from Cheddar's. She thought it would be fairly easy to talk her sister into eating there since it wasn't too far from her place and they offered such a big variety. Maybe they should go to the movies afterwards. They had nothing better to do that night besides sit around and make small talk while they both worried about the small hard knot in Abigail's breast. Something funny, that's what they needed. They would see what was on and either see the funniest thing they could find on or the scariest. Abigail didn't like to be scared as much as Bailey did, but if there wasn't anything funny on, then scary it would be.

By the time Bailey got to Abigail's apartment, Abigail's skin was starting to unshrivel from her long hot bath. She was feeling very relaxed and calm. The girl's went and got a bite to eat and then found a comedy on at the movies. The sheer stupidity of the movie made it all that much more funny to the girls. It was one of those times when they found more humor in the lack of humor more than anything. When they returned home the past few weeks were catching up with them so they decided to make a short night of it. Neither of them got a very good night's sleep, thinking of what was to come. They tried to think positive, that was just hard to do at times.

The next morning both girls were very quiet. Bailey was trying her hardest to stay upbeat for Abigail, but her strength was running low. They went and walked around the mall trying to pass the time before Abigail's appointment at two o'clock, but neither was much in the mood for shopping, a first for Bailey.

Bailey fidgeted and flipped through every magazine they had in the doctor's office while waiting for her sister to emerge from the back. It seemed like it was taking forever, even though it had only been about forty-five minutes. She paced back and forth, got her a cup of coffee, and sat in the corner of the waiting room and prayed. She had always known that God would never put more on her than she could handle, but He was getting really close with this.

Dr. Adams sent a nurse out to bring Bailey back to his office where Abigail was waiting. When Bailey was seated next to her sister and the two were settled, Dr. Adams let out a deep sigh.

"You were right to come in as soon as you found this, Abigail." Abigail felt like she had been weighted down with lead. Bailey reached over and took her sister's hand. "I'll have to do a biopsy, of course," he continued, "to be sure exactly what we're dealing with, but from what I've seen I would say that it is cancerous."

Bailey fought hard to not be sick. She had to be strong for her sister. Her mind was void of all awareness, even though she knew the doctor was still talking.

"It doesn't appear to have spread, but we'll have to check the lymph nodes and make sure. I've got my nurses calling and scheduling the surgery right now. The sooner we get that part over with, the sooner we'll know what course of action we'll need to take."

Abigail was surprisingly calm. She couldn't explain it, but she just knew that everything was going to be okay.

"Bailey," Dr. Adams said, "given your family's history, I would suggest that you get a mammogram as a precautionary, also."

Bailey just stared with wide eyes. She thought she nodded in agreement, but she wasn't really sure if there was a connection between her thoughts and her body right now. "Please, God," she cried out silently, "You can't take my sister from me now. I need her too badly."

The nurse came in and conferred with the doctor for a minute and then gave Abigail a sympathetic look as she walked out of the room. Dr. Adams told them that the surgery procedure would be done first thing Thursday morning. He also told her he would like for her to think of some different options before then. Most likely they would be doing a lumpectomy Thursday, but he thought it might be wise to go ahead and consider having a mastectomy given her mother's history and now her own dealings with this disease. He would, of course, see what they were dealing with first, but better to have thought out everything before going under in case it turned out to be worse than what they were expecting. The two girls just sat there listening, barely comprehending his words.

Bailey shook as she drove them back to her sister's apartment. She had held back the nausea, so far, but wasn't sure how much longer she could do that. She was afraid to speak, but took several glances at Abigail who was in the passenger's seat just staring out the window.

Abigail was surprised at her emotions right now. She was scared, but there was this peace that had washed over her in the doctor's office. She knew right then and there that God was with her no matter what came and she would get through this. She could tell that Bailey was not feeling that same peace right now. She would have to somehow try to convey to her sister what she was feeling and help her gain peace about the situation. She wasn't sure what to do about Patrick. Should they call him and tell him what was happening or wait until they found out more on Thursday? She knew he would be mad at her for not telling him, but she didn't want him to worry about her. She would let Bailey help her with that decision later. Right now she just felt very drained.

## Chapter 48

It felt strange for Sarah to be in this small apartment by herself, but she would get used to it. She had heard from the hospital today and she would have her orientation next week and then start there the following week. She was excited about the thought of her new job. She knew there would be heartbreaking cases that she would have to deal with, but not spend twenty-four hours a day for months with the same person, learning to love them and then have them taken from you. She had requested the pediatrics floor, but she wouldn't know for sure where she would be placed until her orientation. She now had the rest of the week to work on getting a few things for her apartment and getting settled in before going to work. Patrick had already asked if he could take her out on a real date this coming Friday. She had no idea what that would entail, but she was excited to find out. This man that she had spent fourteen months trying to keep at bay had somehow slipped into her heart, and she was thrilled.

Patrick had one thing on his mind today, Sarah. He wanted their first date to be something that she would remember forever. It wasn't so much that he wanted to impress her, but that he wanted her to know how special

# No Regrets

she was to him. He had talked to his dad this morning and had planned for his dad to come down in two weeks. Patrick would be taking a couple of classes the second summer session, but for now he would have time to spend with his dad, and Sarah, and his sisters. Once he started school it would change his way of life drastically for a while. He had never been much of a student and these classes would require his full attention and hours of studying. But for now, it was time for fishing.

Bailey and Abigail were back at the apartment and Abigail had gone to lay down for a nap. Bailey played with the cat for a bit, but needed some air. She took off for a walk and ended up over fourteen blocks away. She ran across a small park and found herself sitting in the small swings, with tears running down her face.

"It's not fair, God." she said out loud. "You know how much I need her. You just have to make this work out okay."

"Is everything okay?"

Bailey jumped as she turned to see this man standing slightly behind her and to her left. "Yes, everything's fine, thank you," she said, wiping her face, embarrassed to have someone listen in on her conversation. Then again, if she hadn't been talking out loud, he wouldn't have heard.

"I didn't mean to startle you," he said. "My name is Luke." He held out his hand as he came around and sat in the swing next to her.

She half-heartedly shook his hand and said, "I'm Bailey."

"I don't mean to intrude," Luke said, "but I couldn't help notice that you looked like you could use a friend."

"I'm fine," she said staring off in the other direction. Who was this man that thought he could just sit down and butt into her business?

"I didn't mean to offend you." He could tell that she hadn't taken warmly to his intrusion. "I heard you talking to God," he pushed on. "I don't know what your situation is, but I can promise you that He will take care of you if you'll let Him."

Bailey's face softened a little bit at his words. "I've always believed that, Luke," she said, "but I'm growing so tired. What happens if I don't have the strength to continue?"

He looked at her with his chocolate brown eyes and said, "Then He'll carry you the rest of the way."

They sat and talked for a while longer. She was feeling a little better about things when she left, but knew whatever came next on Thursday would not be an easy road to walk for any of them. Luke asked if could call her sometime as she was leaving. She didn't normally give her phone number to people she just met, but she could tell by the way he had talked the past hour that he had a close relationship to God. He told her that he would be praying for her and her sister and would call to check to see how the surgery went Thursday.

The fourteen blocks seemed much longer on the way back home, but at least her heart was lighter. Just sharing everything with someone who wasn't personally involved helped her get her perspective back on the situation. She was scared, but she would turn it over to God. He knew what they had been through and how much more they could take. He was in control. When she got back to the apartment Abigail was still asleep. Bailey stretched out on the couch to take her own nap until

# No Regrets

Abigail woke up. Sleep came fast, as did dreams of the stranger named Luke.

As the sister's talked that night they realized that they couldn't keep this from Patrick. They didn't want him to worry, but if the surgery ended up more serious than they hoped, he would be very upset with them for keeping this from him. They called him after they had eaten the pizza they had ordered in was completely devoured. They hadn't realized just how hungry they were. Both had just picked at their lunch.

Abigail thought it best that she talk to Patrick because Bailey almost got sick every time she talked about it. He asked all kinds of questions and Abigail answered them the best she could, but the truth was, she didn't know much right now. She did know that she had decided to go ahead with a mastectomy if the doctor thought it was necessary. The idea of giving up her breast was a horrible feeling, but the idea of dying now or even in the future because of vanity was an even worse thought. Patrick was wanting to leave right then to be with her, but Abigail was able to convince him to wait until Thursday. There was nothing that could be done right now and if he waited he could stay here at her apartment with Bailey instead of getting a hotel room. Abigail would not be needing her bed for sure Thursday night, and maybe even longer. The three prayed together before they hung up and Patrick said that he would call Sarah and tell her the news.

The two sisters were so tired from not sleeping the past few nights that sleep came a little easier tonight. Tomorrow they would make sure that Abigail had everything she needed or that might make her trip to the hospital a little more comfortable.

# Chapter 49

Wednesday seemed to drag on forever for Patrick. He started many times to jump in his truck and head to Abigail's, but they had told him to wait until tomorrow. Tomorrow. His mind was reeling with all the what ifs of tomorrow. He was going to church tonight with Sarah, maybe he would talk to Pastor Tim and get him to pray with him. Patrick really needed some strength and encouragement in his new found faith right now. He and Sarah had stayed on the phone last night for two hours crying together and praying together. He had never had a relationship like that. All the others had left him empty. This one left him feeling complete. Sarah would go up with him tomorrow. She might have to drive back by herself on Sunday, depending on how things went with Abigail. Her new job wouldn't wait. She would be starting Monday no matter what.

Abigail and Bailey went and got pedicures first thing Wednesday morning. They decided that was a definite necessity for Abigail's hospital stay, not to mention that the pampering helped keep their spirits up. Abigail

## No Regrets

wished she would've thought about saving back some of mother's bed jackets, but no one would've ever thought last week that she would need them. Bailey was going to make sure that she found some. No one ever felt comfortable sitting up in the hospital bed in those flimsy gowns. That simply would not do for Bailey's sister. Bailey also made sure her sister had plenty of good smelling lotions and a new candle that she could burn at night to relax her and a new classical music cd. What her sister got out of that music she'd never know, but if it was what she liked, then that's what she would get. Abigail finally had to make Bailey stop buying stuff when she realized she was even buying mints and potpourri for her bedside table. After all, she wasn't moving in. Hopefully, she would just be there for a few days. They took everything back to the apartment and left the sacks in the living room. They could pack when they got home from church tonight. Abigail hadn't really felt like going to church and being around everyone, but she couldn't stand to pass up the opportunity to have others pray over her. She wanted every prayer warrior she knew going to war with her on this. She had to survive. She wasn't ready to leave this world when she felt like she had just begun to live.

Patrick would have put his sister on the prayer list that evening at church, but he couldn't bear to face the sympathetic looks and all the questions people would ask and the hugs. He would just talk to Pastor Tim privately afterwards, and then Pastor Tim could call the prayer chain. When he got home from church he called Abigail to talk to her before she went to bed. No one would be getting much sleep tonight, but he wanted her to at least try to rest. He told her they would leave early in the morning and try to be there before they took her back. They talked for a bit about the decisions she had made in case there were more serious things that needed to be done. It broke his heart to be talking about this with his sister. They had become so much closer through their mother's illness. He was having a hard time figuring out how all of this was God's will. There would be a lot of tossing and turning and praying going on throughout the night.

## Chapter 50

Patrick and Sarah made it to the hospital just before Dr. Adams came into the room to talk with them. Abigail told him of her decisions and gave him permission to remove one or both of her breasts, if necessary. She didn't want to have to go through another surgery if she didn't have to. He went over all that he would be doing today, anything that they might have to do, what to expect with the anesthesia, all of the normal pre-surgery check lists. He also made sure that he explained all of the reconstructive surgery that was available should she have to have the mastectomy. Abigail wasn't really concerned with that at this point, in fact, that had never crossed her mind. She was primarily concerned with making sure she lived right now. The extra gentle way that Dr. Adams talked to Abigail didn't go unnoticed by Bailey.

Dr. Adams assured them that he would come out and talk to them as soon as he knew anything and then left to prepare for the surgery. The nurse came and gave Abigail something in her IV to make her groggy.

"At least someone will finally get some rest around

here," Bailey teased.

Bailey, Patrick, and Sarah prayed one last time with Abigail and then each gave her a kiss. They watched as she was wheeled away.

Bailey was not good at waiting. She was driving Patrick crazy with her pacing and sitting and standing and flipping through magazines and tapping her foot. He finally got up and went down the hall and stepped outside where they had set up a smoking area. There was no one out here right now, so the air was semi-fresh. It seemed horrible compared to the air back in Criar, but he felt like he was suffocating in that small, dark waiting room.

Sarah was good with Bailey. She had the patience to let her roam like a caged lion, and a voice that helped sooth her. This was what she was used to, helping people cope with facing serious illness. She had faith that Abigail wasn't dying, but when you have a loved one in there on that table, it almost hurts just as bad. Sarah tried to talk to the nurses a few times, see if she could find anything out, but no one would tell her anything except that the doctor would be out to talk to them shortly. Shortly turned into four hours later. Sarah walked down to where Patrick had gone outside and called him in to come talk to Dr. Adams.

They all sat down with Dr. Adams in a corner of the waiting room. They couldn't tell by the expression on his face if he was just tired from the surgery or if things weren't good. They hoped he was just tired.

"The tumor was definitely cancerous. There were other cells starting to form throughout both of her breasts, but her lymph nodes were clear. We had to do a double mastectomy. We could've tried to save them, but with her family history, I really don't feel like it would've been worth the risk. If it comes back, it will come back with a vengeance."

"So the surgery took care of everything?" asked Bailey.

"Well," he continued, "we will still need to go through a round of chemotherapy to ensure that we haven't missed any cells."

"Chemotherapy?" said Patrick.

"Yes," said Dr. Adams. "We will let her body heal a bit before we start the treatments, so that her immune system will be strong enough to handle it, but then we will get with the Oncologist and let them set up a course of treatment."

Bailey wasn't sure she understood what he was saying completely. "So when the treatments are over, she'll be fine?" she asked.

"I feel strongly that between the surgery today and the chemotherapy treatments that she'll be fine, but we won't know for certain until after the treatments come and go, and we run more tests to make sure we got it all." He explained this in a way that sounded as if this was all just a simple procedure. "She will be in recovery for about another half hour or so and then they will be taking her back to her room. I'll be stopping by to make sure she is okay and to answer any questions you might have. I'll also be sure to come and talk to Abigail when she wakes up enough to remember what I say."

"Thank you, Dr. Adams," Patrick said, still unsure about a few things, but too confused to know what questions to ask right now. There would be time for that later.

They went upstairs to Abigail's room to wait for her to be brought back. She was still pretty out of it and continued to doze off seconds after she would open her eyes and see them. They came to the conclusion that there was nothing else they could do for her right now, except be there. She looked so weak and frail laying there in the bed with all the bandages. They were trying not to let images of their mother lying in bed be conjured up in their imagination. They would have to put that behind them for now and focus on Abigail's future, not their past.

That night when Dr. Adams came back in he told them that he had arranged for an Oncologist to come by and talk to Abigail in the next couple of days. She would probably be in the hospital at least another three days and then it would be another week or so before they would start the treatments.

Patrick sent Bailey and Sarah back to the apartment that night and volunteered to stay with Abigail since he really didn't have anywhere to go yet. He spent most of the night just staring at his sister, remembering how much she had taken care of him while growing up. He couldn't imagine how hard that must have been for her, but he was thankful to her for all she had done. Every time he would doze off, it seemed, the nurses would be coming in and out to check on Abigail. He would be glad when morning came.

The next couple of days in the hospital consisted of a lot of sitting and waiting for Bailey, Patrick, and Sarah, and a lot of sleeping for Abigail. She was in great pain most of the time, but had accepted the outcome of the surgery with resolution. She was more apprehensive about the chemotherapy than she was the surgery. She could handle being sick during that time to save her own life, but she was scared to death of losing her hair. Had

## No Regrets

Dr. Adams, or Brian, as he had asked her to call him, really meant the comment that she would be just as beautiful without hair as she was with hair, or had that been the pain medicine affecting her hearing? The Oncologist came by and discussed in detail with Abigail what the treatments would consist of and that they would like to do one treatment a week for three months and see if that would take care of things.

"Three months," she kept telling herself, "she could handle that."

# Chapter 51

The next few months were a whirlwind of activity. Bailey had decided to commute from Abigail's house as much as possible so that she could be there for her sister. Sarah would come down and relieve her on the weekends so that she could go home and take care of bills and just get away for a little bit, and Patrick would relieve them every once in a while when he could. School had started for him, so they wanted him to focus on that, and he was still trying to have his visits with his dad every couple of weeks. They had really been able to get to know each other a little better and were feeling more like father and son than strangers. It would still take time, but wounds were healing.

Abigail really had a hard time with the chemotherapy. She was sick most all of the time and as expected, she lost her hair. Bailey had cut her hair super short when the first sign of hair started showing up on her pillow and in the sink when she would brush her hair, but the actual loss of it was very hard on Abigail. Bailey had also found her all types of cute turbans and hats that the cancer society makes available to cancer patients. Some were so silly that she had to give Abigail a little push to wear them, but they would always end up laughing and enjoying the silliness in such hard times. Bailey was good at keeping the laughter close at hand when they needed it most. They had become so much more than sisters over the past couple of months, they were best friends. They had even talked about them moving a little closer to each other. They could move somewhere more in the middle of where they each were now and commute. They would rather have to drive a little bit and be able to see each other more.

Sarah and Patrick had fallen head over heels in the first month of dating. Patrick had asked her to marry him their sixth week together and she readily accepted the proposal. They would have the wedding when Spring came back around at the house in Criar. Abigail and Bailey couldn't have been happier to have Sarah join their family. They loved her as a sister and knew that she would be a wonderful wife for their brother.

They had survived more than any of them ever thought they would have the strength to survive. They had no regrets of where they had been, because it had led them to where they now were. It took their lives almost falling apart to realize that God was always in control and holding them together. They had their mother to thank for that. Her life was a testimony to them that they would pass on to their children someday. They now realized how much of a testimony their own lives could be to others.

# Epilogue

Patrick was shaking as he stood under the garden trellis that had been brought in for the wedding. The yard was absolutely running over with pink and white roses and lilies. It had been exactly one year since his mother had died in this very house, and one year ago he could've never imagined himself wanting to spend the rest of his life with one woman, but Sarah was different. She was sent to him and his family by God, Himself, and he would treasure her as the rare and beautiful gift that he knew she was.

He watched with tears in his eyes as his sister, Abigail, came down the aisle on the arm of the man that had helped save her life in the operating room. They were forever grateful to Dr. Brian Adams and the care he had shown their sister as a physician and as a friend. Abigail's hair had grown back, but she had chosen to wear in an adorable pixie cut. Patrick really liked it that way, even though he teased her horribly about her hair being shorter than his.

Next to come down the aisle was his sister, Bailey. She had proved to be a woman of incredible strength and devotion. She had been considered pretty much the flighty one or the class clown of the family, but the way she stood up and took control when Abigail fell sick was amazing. She was on the arm of Luke, the man she calls her angel from the park. He had been a great support to all of them during the time of Abigail's hospitalization and chemotherapy. He stayed out of everyone's way most of the time, but you could always feel the prayers coming from his direction. And if he could put up with Bailey, that was an added bonus.

As the string quartet started playing the wedding march and Patrick saw Sarah emerge from the house, he wasn't sure if he could continue standing. He had never seen a more beautiful woman in his life. Not only was she beautiful, but she was a woman that loved God even more than the man she was now marrying. He found her devotion to God absolutely inspiring and it made him want to be the man of God that she deserved. What was even more amazing to Patrick was that she was on the arm of his own father. A man that he hadn't known up until the day of his mother's funeral almost a year ago. He could've never imagined forgiving this man for walking out on him before birth, until he learned of forgiveness for himself. Another thing their mother had shown them. He looked at the man he now called dad and knew in his heart that he had no regrets.

Printed in the United States
38101LVS00002B/283-387